THE BRIDES OF BELLA ROSA

Romance, rivalry and a family reunited.

For years Lisa Firenze and Luca Casali's
sibling rivalry has disturbed the quiet,
sleepy Italian town of Monta Correnti,
and their two feuding restaurants
have divided the market square.

Now, as the keys to the restaurants are handed
down to Lisa's and Luca's children, will history
repeat itself? Can the next generation undo
its parents' mistakes, reunite the families
and ultimately join the two restaurants?

Or are there more secrets to be revealed…?

*The doors to the restaurants are open,
so take your seats and look out for secrets,
scandals and surprises on the menu!*

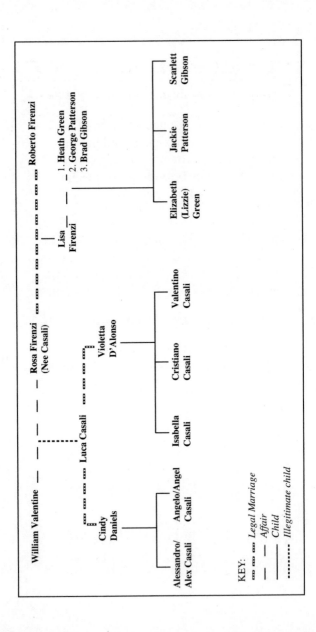

William Valentine

Rosa Firenzi (Nee Casali)

Roberto Firenzi

Luca Casali

Lisa Firenzi

1. Heath Green
2. George Patterson
3. Brad Gibson

Cindy Daniels

Violetta D'Alonso

Elizabeth (Lizzie) Green

Jackie Patterson

Scarlett Gibson

Alessandro/ Alex Casali

Angelo/Angel Casali

Isabella Casali

Cristiano Casali

Valentino Casali

KEY:

▬ ▬ ▬ *Legal Marriage*

▬ ▬ *Affair*

⎯⎯ *Child*

·········· *Illegitimate child*

MIRACLE FOR THE GIRL NEXT DOOR

BY
REBECCA WINTERS

MILLS & BOON

First published in Great Britain 2010
Harlequin Mills & Boon Limited,
Eton House, 18-24 Paradise Road, Richmond, Surrey TW9 1SR

© Harlequin Books S.A. 2010

Special thanks and acknowledgement are given to Rebecca Winters for her contribution to The Brides of Bella Rosa series.

ISBN: 978 0 263 21363 8

Rebecca Winters, whose family of four children has now swelled to include five beautiful grandchildren, lives in Salt Lake City, Utah, in the land of the Rocky Mountains. With canyons and high Alpine meadows full of wild flowers, she never runs out of places to explore. They, plus her favourite vacation spots in Europe, often end up as backgrounds for her Mills & Boon® Romance novels, because writing is her passion, along with her family and church.

Rebecca loves to hear from her readers. If you wish to e-mail her, please visit her website at www.cleanromances.com

To my one and only
darling daughter Dominique Jessop,
who recently signed her first book contract with
Harlequin. Her study experience abroad in Siena, Italy,
has caused her to become a lover of all things Italian,
just like her mother. With her input on Limoncello,
my Mills & Boon® Romance novel
MIRACLE FOR THE GIRL NEXT DOOR
has been enriched.

CHAPTER ONE

CLARA ROSSETTI had started to descend the steep, narrow steps between the ancient buildings of the hillside town when she heard a deep male voice behind her say, "Hey, Bella—how many men have told you you're a remarkably beautiful woman?"

His seductive delivery had been spoken in the local Italian dialect and had a slightly familiar ring. But Clara assumed he had to be talking to some other female making her way down to the Piazza Gaspare below.

Picking up her pace, she moved across the busy square to the bus stop where she would catch her bus. It would be the last one of the day. Timing was everything when she felt this tired. Once back at the farm she would eat a light dinner and go to bed. Tomorrow she'd feel better.

Footsteps were gaining on her. "Clarissima—surely you haven't forgotten!"

A quiet gasp escaped her throat followed by a burst of joy. *Tino*.

After nine years' absence her best friend from childhood was back? Valentino Casali was the only person in the world who'd ever called her Clarissima—a combination of Clara and *bellissima*. Clara had often thought it a joke since from adolescence she had been a chubby girl who'd grown into a heavy young woman. That was the curse of all the Rossettis.

She turned around to stare into the flashing dark brown eyes of Europe's most eligible playboy, but to Clara he represented her exclusive partner in all the craziness of their years growing up. When they'd both turned eighteen and he'd left Monta Correnti, his departure had left a void no one else had ever filled.

Since then he'd become Italy's poster boy, a wealthy, world-renowned adventurer and playboy whose photos appeared in the tabloids on a regular basis. He was constantly on the cover of Italy's hottest celebrity gossip magazine.

"No, I haven't forgotten," she said in a husky voice. Clara had seen him through every stage of his youth, from incorrigible rascal to outrageously handsome teen. His intelligence and daring had distinguished him from all the other guys in the region, leaving an indelible mark. To her he'd always been the picture of precious life itself. Her heart groaned in response to that undeniable reality. "How are you, Valentino?"

Her question seemed to bring him up short, as if he were expecting something else from her while he stared into her eyes. "Better now that I've caught up with my oldest friend."

Delight filled her system to hear him acknowledge it. He might belong to the world now, but those early years she could claim for herself.

After he had kissed her on both cheeks, his narrowed gaze traveled over her classic features as if trying to reconcile the changes that had taken place since she'd grown up and become the slender, five-foot-four woman who'd shed the excess weight she had carried when younger.

"Friend, you say?" she teased. "Whatever happened to the postcards and gifts from the four corners of the world you were going to send me? I don't recall your carrying out any of those periodic visits you once promised to make."

He gave an elegant shrug of his broad shoulders clothed in an expensive-looking open-necked cream sport shirt and jeans. His index finger trailed across her lips, a gesture that appeared as automatic to him as breathing, but he'd never touched her like that in their lives. A shock wave traveled through her body.

"I meant to do it all. You know that," he whispered, always the charmer. The man oozed a sensuality that would be lethal for the many women clamoring for his exclusive attention.

She flashed him a wan smile, struggling to recover from her reaction to his touch. "I *do* know. Your good intentions could pave the road to heaven." Their history went back too far for there to be misunderstandings. In truth Clara could never be angry with the Valentino she remembered—the one who'd always been kind and caring despite his devil-may-care attitude.

From an early age on, the local *ragazzi* had made their typical remarks about her and her younger sister Bianca for being fat, but Valentino had never joined the chorus. That was probably because he'd never looked at her in the man/woman way. They might have been joined at the hip, but he'd had far more important things on his mind than Clara Rossetti.

Having been born in this quiet little mountain village between Rome and Naples, he'd put Monta Correnti on the map. His fame had brought the tourists, as well as a few celebrities from various parts of the world who'd chosen to live here, but there was no question that the heartthrob Formula 1 race-car driver who made his home in Monaco was the most famous celebrity of all.

Valentino cocked his attractive head. She noted he needed a shave, yet it only added to his virility. In the last nine years, he'd become a man in every sense of the word and so gorgeous she could hardly breathe.

"Are you aware you bear a superficial resemblance to Catherine Zeta-Jones? Only younger, of course."

Clara preferred not to look like anyone else, but since film stars made up part of his world she had to assume he'd just bestowed a serious compliment on her. "No. I had no idea. Have you met her?"

He gave a slight nod. "You're much more beautiful." His white smile faded and he stared at her with increasing intensity. "What happened to your long hair?"

The hair she'd foolishly hoped would hide the rest of her?

Surprised he'd noticed, let alone changed the subject so fast, she said, "This April has been warmer than usual. Besides, I was due for a change." Her silky hair, more black than brown, had become too difficult to deal with recently so she'd had it cut in a jaw-length style that fell straight from a center part.

"I liked it long, not that I don't like it the way you're wearing it now, of course."

"Of course," she teased, wishing she felt better, stronger. "I notice you're wearing your hair shorter these days." His midnight-brown hair was now wavy rather than curly. "Remember when you let it grow out to your shoulders? Signor Cavallo thought you'd be perfect for the role of Prince Valiant in the school play."

A rumble of laughter came out of him. "Are you talking about the time you denuded me?"

"That was *your* fault. You're the one who made me cut your hair off so you wouldn't have to be in *King Arthur*. Can I help it if I made a mess of it? Those poultry shears from your father's restaurant kitchen weren't supposed to be used on humans. I thought Signor Cavallo was going to strangle you when you walked in class the next day."

His grin broadened. "With your help, I got out of the part. What would I have done without you always helping me squeeze out of trouble?"

"Aminta almost strangled me when you told her I was the

culprit. She had the most terrible crush on you. Even back then you could have your choice of every maiden in the land."

"Tonight I choose you," he said in a voice of deep velvet. "For old times' sake, come to the restaurant with me and we'll celebrate my return."

"To sneak some *bruschetta* when the chef isn't looking?" She kept up the banter. There was no one more exciting in this world than Valentino. "Those were the days, but we can't get them back."

"No, but there's something we *can* do. Tonight's your lucky night. For a change we'll walk through the front door and I'll *buy* you dinner. Everything up front and aboveboard."

His invitation sounded heavenly, but she was growing weaker by the minute. "That would be a change all right, but, much as I'd love to, I can't. Thank you anyway. It's been wonderful to see you, Valentino."

Over his shoulder she saw the bus pull to a stop. She was thankful it had come to her rescue. Seeing Valentino after all these years had brought back the past and drained her of any reserves she had left. Several people started to board the bus and she moved to get in line behind them.

He put a hand on her arm to detain her. "Wait—where are you going?" She discovered a strange tension coming from him she'd never experienced before. Something was troubling him to produce that slight grimace, but she had to admit the years had been kind to him. Despite the lines of experience in a sun-bronzed face—or perhaps because of them—he was more dashing than ever. No other man came close.

"Home. The family's waiting for me."

"But I just got into town. We have years to catch up on. Is this evening an important occasion? I know it's not your birthday."

He might have forgotten *her* for nine years, but his razor-sharp memory had an amazing capacity for trivia. Valentino would keep it up until she capitulated. He never did know when to quit, but this was one time Clara couldn't stay around while he managed to talk her into it. She was embarrassed to admit he'd always been able to get her to do what he wanted.

"Mamma has planned a special dinner for my grandmother. I promised to be on time to help."

Again he looked mystified. "Then let me drive you. It will only take me five minutes to go for my Ferrari."

That was too far away. Clara needed to sit down on that bus or she was going to faint from exhaustion. "Thanks for the offer, but my ride is here now. If you're going to be in town for a few days, maybe I'll see you whizzing around and we'll grab a bite together. What color is your car?"

"Black," he muttered.

"You once wanted a red one."

"I did buy one, fire-engine red, but discovered I was somewhat a target for the police."

"Well, you *will* insist on driving too fast. As I recall, you had the police chasing us on your scooter on a weekly basis at least! Sorry, but I have to run now. *Ciao*, Valentino."

She eased away from him and climbed on board, grateful he'd finally let her go without saying anything else. Knowing him, he'd be gone from Monta Correnti by morning to make his next car rally here in Italy or England, probably accompanied by his latest girlfriend.

Clara had seen a clip of him and the newest young French starlet Giselle Artois on the ten o'clock news last month. The journalist had asked him if it was true about the rumors they were planning to marry and settle down in a small palace along one of the fashionable *faubourgs* of Paris.

He had made a noncommittal remark with his breathtaking half-smile, but Clara had noticed the French *vedette* wore a mysterious smile on her face. They looked good together.

Maybe this was the woman who'd finally snagged Valentino. Up until now he seemed to try new adventures and change girl-friends with the seasons, but whatever had caused him to run from himself all these years, it was nothing to do with Clara.

Taking a fortifying breath, she worked her way to the back of the bus. Every seat was taken and she finally squeezed in the last row between a stout man and a nun in her habit.

Out of the window on the right she watched Valentino watching her beneath his dark, furrowed brows, his expression devoid of all animation. After the bus pulled away, his brooding image remained. His lean, six-foot body had made millions for the companies that produced posters of him doing a solo trip across the Indian Ocean in a one-man catamaran, or flying around the track in Dubai testing out his latest Formula 1 car.

From childhood he'd been a fascinating adventurer who'd had an obsession with speed and breaking records. Though the Casali family had lived on the shores of Lake Clarissa, fifty kilometers from Monta Correnti, he'd actually spent most of his time in town after school working on his motor scooter.

One of his friends, Luigi, had let him tinker with it in the back of his dad's garage. To hear Valentino speak, none of the existing models were fast enough. Clara had spent many hours in that garage listening to him talk about his dreams of building one that would outperform all existing models.

After he'd left for Monaco to break into the racing world, he'd taken his innovative motor-scooter design with him and it had become the prototype for future scooters. By his twenty-first birthday he'd formed Violetta Rapidita, the Italian scooter company that had catapulted him to international financial success.

Long ago Clara had thought of him as a Renaissance man, pitting himself against the clock, against nature, against anything that would give him a thrill. By listening to him she'd experienced vicarious thrills herself, but there were times when she wondered if his fast living served as camouflage for unexplained demons driving him.

Though she didn't know what they were, she suspected their roots originated from within the complicated Casali family and that they still continued to haunt him. It was interesting that his elder brother Cristiano didn't come home to Monta Correnti very often either.

Only their sister Isabella had been the constant, spending most of her time at Rosa's helping her father run the restaurant. How different was Valentino's family from the huge, hard-working Rossetti clan who always rallied around each other!

She had countless aunts, uncles, cousins and second cousins who helped run the farm, so many in fact you couldn't count them all. Though they lived hand to mouth, even her own four married siblings showed no signs of leaving the farm that had been the hub of the Rossettis' existence for generations.

Clara was no different. As hard as life had been lately, she loved Monta Correnti and couldn't imagine living anywhere else. But fate had been cruel to have allowed her to lay eyes on Valentino today.

Until he'd called out to her, she'd been holding her own, dealing with her challenges on a day-to-day basis, determined not to let them defeat her. But he was like this overpowering force field, a super-bright constellation in the heavens whose magnetic pull drew the world to him.

His appearance had managed to shatter the fragile shell of her existence. She rested her head against the back of the seat and closed her eyes, tortured by her own inner demons that seemed to have magnified a hundredfold by running into him without warning.

* * *

The second the bus rounded the corner and was out of sight, a troubled Valentino moved swiftly toward the hub of the village where his father's restaurant was located. Right next to it—in fact adjoining it by a back terrace—sat his aunt's restaurant. The courtyard in front of both opened up into the bustling center square.

Sorella, a restaurant started by Valentino's grandmother Rosa, was now owned by his aunt Lisa Firenzi who'd turned it into a chic, contemporary place serving an international cuisine. His father, Luca Casali, had fallen out with his sister and had broken away from the family business, starting his own Italian traditional family restaurant he'd named Rosa. Isabella was the day manager.

Valentino had kept in touch with her and their father through e-mails, but in the last nine years he'd only come home fleetingly. The most recent had been just last month on the occasion of his father's birthday. Much to his sister's chagrin he'd only stayed the evening.

Just remembering that fateful evening and the fireworks that had ensued caused him to shudder. He always experienced an unpleasant sensation in his gut at the thought that two warring factions of the same family would want to be anywhere near each other. Valentino abhorred confrontation and was continually mystified that two intelligent people like his father and his aunt Lisa, who'd had a jealous rivalry going for years, still maintained businesses side by side.

It was a sick kind of symbiosis. They were like organisms surviving in close approximation, not able to live with or without the other.

As he reached the courtyard he was reminded of the ugly confrontation that had gone on out here during the party. Tempers had flared. Uncaring of who might overhear them, his aunt had lost control. In her rage she'd blurted out a sensitive secret about Luca that had rocked the entire family.

Pain had gutted Valentino. Unable to deal with all the ramifications, not the least of which was his bitter disappointment in his father, he'd left Monta Correnti after having barely arrived not knowing when he'd ever be back. If it weren't for his father's declining health and Isabella's plea for help with him, Valentino wouldn't have canceled his next two races to be here now.

However, his overriding concern tonight had nothing to do with his father. After leaving the furnished villa he'd just rented at the upper end of the village, he'd been making his way down to the restaurant on foot, never dreaming he would run into Clara Rossetti within hours of arriving back in town.

Their chance meeting had saved him the trouble of looking her up at the farm. The knowledge that he could reconnect with her while he was in Monta Correnti had been the only thing he'd been looking forward to on his return.

Clara had been his saving grace, had always accepted him with his flaws and imperfections. After the party he'd needed desperately to talk to her about what he'd learned, but he'd been in such bad shape at the time he hadn't been willing to inflict himself on her.

He wasn't doing much better now, but seeing her again made him realize how much he wanted to talk to her. There was no one as insightful or as easy to be with as Clara. No one understood him the way she did, but at first glance he hadn't recognized her except for her eyes.

Those incredible irises studded with luminous, diamond-like green dust hadn't changed though everything else about her had. Gone was the overweight teenager with the pretty face who'd been his abiding friend since they'd first attended school as children. In her place stood a gorgeous woman, albeit a little too thin, no longer hidden beneath a cascading veil of glossy dark hair. Just looking at her amazing coloring and figure stopped him in his tracks.

But more startling was the fact that, beyond the drastic alteration in her physical appearance, she didn't radiate that joie de vivre he'd thought inherent in her nature.

Instead of crying out 'Tino', the name she used to call him, she'd proffered the more formal greeting of his name, treating him as she might a former acquaintance. In reality they'd been partners in crime, doing everything together, getting in and out of trouble on a regular basis.

The old fun-loving Clara, always ready for a new adventure, wouldn't have gotten on that bus.

Maybe she was telling the truth and did have to get home, but something had been missing. She'd said all the right words, yet the warm, compassionate girl he'd turned to in his youth— the one person who'd always listened to him and had never scoffed at his bold ideas—had put him off.

That had come as a shock.

He'd been arrogant enough to believe in some corner of his mind that, of all the people who'd come and gone in his life, she'd placed their friendship on a higher par—or at least on a unique plane that meant it was something special, even if he hadn't written letters or sent her pictures. It seemed she didn't want to spend time with him now.

With the Rossettis' farm of lemon, orange and olive groves located several miles south of town, the formerly vivacious Clara wouldn't have turned him down for a ride home. He'd never known a woman who didn't want to take a jaunt with him in his Ferrari. Valentino supposed his ego was hurt that she wasn't impressed, let alone that her memories of him had made no lasting mark on her psyche.

Her dark-fringed eyes might have flared with interest when she'd first seen him, but as they had talked it had felt as if she were staring through him, making him feel at a loss. That spark of life he'd always associated with her had been missing, delivering a one-two punch to the gut he hadn't expected. In truth, he had to reach back to being five years old again to remember that same sensation, leaving him feeling devastated.

He quickened his pace and hurried inside the restaurant where the staff was setting up for dinner. They called out greetings he acknowledged, but he was in too big a hurry to get engaged in conversation. Without hesitation he headed toward the kitchen where his recently engaged sister was probably doing ten tasks at once to keep things running smoothly.

After taking possession of the villa where he planned to live for the next few months, he'd come here with every intention of eating his evening meal, but, after the strange experience with Clara in the piazza, he was now put off the thought of food.

Rosa, named after his grandmother, delivered traditional, home-cooked Italian food in surroundings of frescoed walls and terracotta floors. The rustic restaurant represented his father's dream of owning his own place. He'd wanted it to be evocative of his mother's warm, family-oriented spirit.

In that regard, he hadn't failed. Aside from Clara, who'd made up the best part of the background fabric of his life, Valentino's few good memories included the experience of walking in here to encounter the distinctive aroma of the tomato sauce, Rosa's house specialty, wafting past his nostrils.

William Valentine, his English grandfather, had passed his secret sauce recipe to his sweetheart Rosa who had later passed it on to her son Luca, Valentino's father. Luca had then improved on the recipe, which was the reason for the restaurant's popularity, even if at this point in time he was heavily in debt.

Valentino had the finances to help him out. At Isabella's repeated urgings, he'd come back home for a while to do just that, but the latest revelation about his father made it damn near impossible to want to approach him.

Being back home brought all the painful memories of the past flooding to the surface, one of them still unbearable if he allowed himself to think about it too much. To make matters worse, he had to maneuver carefully because of his father's declining health and fierce pride.

For two cents he'd leave for Monaco tonight and make arrangements to race in the next Grand Prix. But he couldn't do that and disappoint Isabella again. He'd made her a promise to spend time at the restaurant. Tonight he'd talk to her about some ideas he had to promote the business. With a quick fix he could be out of here a lot sooner!

His sister saw him enter the kitchen. A glance from her expressive blue eyes told him she wanted to talk to him. She took her leave of the chef and signaled with her head that Valentino should follow her out the back door to the nearby stream that ran through the town. In recent years it had been cemented into a channel with bridges where they could lean against the railings and talk in private.

"I was hoping you'd get back in time for dinner," she began without preamble. "Are you going to take the villa? It's been empty for ages. Max hoped you might be interested in it."

Valentino nodded. "I told Max I would rent it on a month-to-month basis. It's roomy and the view is great. It's an ideal solution for my temporary situation."

She looked chagrined. "I thought you said the whole summer."

He'd thought so too until his own pride had suffered a debilitating blow from Clara, the one person he would never have imagined could inflict hurt of any kind, not even unconsciously. It surprised him how much he cared. He was a fool to let it bother him, yet it was eating at him like a corrosive acid and he didn't like the feeling.

"You know me. I have an aversion to being pinned down."
Isabella didn't like hearing those words, but she had played
mother to him and Cristiano for so many years, she couldn't
help but try to manage everything, even now.

Once he'd committed to coming home for a while, she'd
insisted he stay at the vacant Casali home on Lake Clarissa now
used for vacations. It was only a half-hour's drive from town.
When she'd first mentioned it, he'd told her it was too far away
to be convenient. In truth, he didn't know if he could ever step
inside that building again. What had happened there so many
years ago would haunt him to the grave.

"I'm sorry you didn't choose to stay in the apartment with
Papa. He was hoping you might move in with him."

Isabella was out of her mind to say something like that. He
swore his sister lived in denial. Her constant desire to make everything right between everybody and get along drove him
around the bend. He was still furious with her for insisting they
get to know their two older half-brothers, Alessandro and
Angelo. Until little more than a month ago, no one in the
family had known of their existence. Unbelievable!

Yet thanks to his trouble-making aunt, Luca's guilty secret
had been exposed and now Isabella was determined to make
them a part of their dysfunctional lives. No, thank you.

"I'm afraid I've been on my own too many years, Izzy.
Besides, let's be honest. You're always looking in on Papa and
don't need a second person being underfoot, even if I am your
brother. Please don't take that the wrong way."

She kissed his cheek. "I didn't."

"I admire you for taking care of him." That part was the
truth. In her own right she was a terrific person. With her long,
wavy black hair and olive skin, he considered her the quintes-
sential Italian woman. "Papa couldn't have made it this long
without you." She'd been the glue holding the family together.

"Thank you," she said in a quiet voice.

"I should have said something long before now." When he saw the work she did without complaint day after day, it made him feel all the more uncomfortable that already today he'd been entertaining thoughts of bolting before morning.

Her eyes searched his. "You're in a strange mood. You burst into the kitchen like you were being pursued, and now you're being uncharacteristically reflective. What happened to you after you talked to Max about the villa?"

Like a mother with eyes in the back of her head, his sister saw more than he wanted her to see. He'd run into Clara Rossetti on the way here, but their unexpected encounter hadn't turned out as he'd anticipated, leaving him strangely unsettled.

"I've had an idea on how to expand the business. Unfortunately Papa is such a traditionalist, I don't know if he'll hear me out. I'm the last person he wants advice from."

"How can you say that?" she cried. "You're an international success in business. You could double your fortune showing others how to make it big."

"That doesn't impress a bona fide restaurateur like Papa."

"Of course it does!"

He shook his head. "Let's not play games, Izzy. *You* know why." They stared at each other. "I'm not his biological son. I'm a reminder that I was Mamma's love child from another man."

"Papa raised you as his own with me and Cristiano."

"Yes, and every time he sees me on television or hears about me on the news, he has to wonder about the stranger who was half responsible for my existence. I gave up caring a long time ago when I realized my birth father didn't want anything to do with me either."

Her soulful eyes looked up at him helplessly.

"If he had, he would have made arrangements with Mamma for visitation. Papa had to take me when he took Mamma back.

After she died, he was stuck with me. Considering he didn't want his first two sons, let's just say the bastard child comes in last on all counts."

"No, Valentino!" She threw her arms around him. "That's not true. You simply can't believe those things."

"Let's not talk about it anymore, Izzy. It's water under the bridge." He didn't want to get into the subject of their father. The shocking revelation that his first marriage had produced two sons living somewhere else on the planet had done too much damage to Valentino. He felt emotionally wiped out. Erased.

Isabella wiped her eyes. "Then tell me about your idea."

"I don't know if it will work, but I think it's worth a try. This establishment has been Papa's dream. None of us wants to see it go under." In Luca's own way he'd been a good father to Valentino. It was payback time.

"We can't let that happen."

"Agreed. What would you think if we did some advertising with various tour-group operators from Rome and Naples to bring in more people? I'll do the groundwork, of course. If it's a go, I'll contact other operators in Florence and Milan."

"That's pure genius!" she cried excitedly.

He shook his head. "Papa will probably hate it. Secondly I'd like to set up an Internet Web site for us. Anyone seeing our name on a restaurant list can contact us to make advance reservations. Once we're set up on the best search engines, we ought to see an increase in traffic."

"Those are both fabulous ideas. Once people discover us, they always come back for repeat business."

"The trick is to get them here. We just need to spread the word. When do you think would be the best time to approach Papa?"

"Mornings, after he's up and dressed for breakfast."

"I'll come tomorrow. Depending on how he's feeling, I'll broach the subject."

"I'm so glad you're here."

Wishing he could say the same, he hugged her instead. Unfortunately being back meant having to face his old ghosts. The fact that Cristiano was in Australia only reminded Valentino how far the Casali family had grown apart emotionally. Which reminded him of something else unpleasant.

"Did I tell you I happened to see Clara Rossetti in the piazza this afternoon?"

"Oh, yes? You two were inseparable growing up. Sometimes I think she was the only person you ever truly cared about after Mamma died. I used to be jealous of her."

He blinked, not only shocked by her admission, but by the fact that his attachment to Clara had been so obvious, his own sister had been affected by it. "I had no idea."

"Of course you wouldn't. I saw her at church recently. She's grown up to be a real beauty."

"I noticed." Maybe it was the weight loss that had affected her behavior and made her seem less than her herself. The way she'd brushed him off had stung.

"Bianca, too. You remember her sister."

"Very well." She was a year younger than Clara and almost as sweet. Too bad he couldn't say the same about Clara's twin brother, Silvio. The Casalis and the Rossettis had attended the same schools, but from the beginning Silvio had taken a distinct dislike to Valentino.

By high school he'd become Clara's self-appointed guardian, doing his best to keep her away from Valentino, always reminding her she was needed back at the farm. Though it had never come to an actual fight, they'd exchanged heated words on occasion when Valentino had stood up for Clara.

"Rumour has it that Clara has been seeing one of the Romaggio brothers from the valley."

So *that* was the reason she'd seemed changed. "Which one?"

"I think it's Leandro, the really good-looking one who has his own vegetable farm now. Apparently Clara is the envy of all the girls around here."

Izzy had to be kidding—Leandro was the one with more brawn than brains. Valentino had known the Romaggios in school. Clara had an intellect that could run circles around any of the guys. He wasn't her type at all!

For some reason the news made Valentino restless. "Thanks for backing me up in my ideas. Now I've got to go. I left Monaco early this morning and fatigue has caught up with me."

"That doesn't surprise me. I need to go back inside, too. The staff will be wondering where I am."

"I'll see you tomorrow." He kissed her cheek before wheeling around to make his own way through the ancient town and up the hillside to the villa.

Valentino hadn't been completely honest with Isabella. After being up since five that morning to drive to Italy, he would normally be tired and wanting his bed. But the old saying that you couldn't go home again seemed to be in operation here. Meeting up with a changed Clara had disturbed him and he found himself wide awake.

Once he reached his destination, he let himself in the villa originally built in the 1800s by a member of Prince Maximilliano Di Rossi's family for a summer getaway. Because of his love for Izzy, Max had made the villa available to Valentino, who had insisted on paying him rent. He didn't like owing anyone for favors. With no strings attached, he could move about freely in his world.

The villa was much smaller but no different in style from Valentino's home in Monaco. Both had been built around the same period of time and contained similar furnishings. The only real difference besides size was the view. It looked out on the picturesque countryside rather than the Mediterranean.

At the sound of his footsteps echoing throughout the interior, Valentino realized that without warm bodies inhabiting this domicile it was nothing more than an empty tomb. Valentino wasn't used to the peace and quiet. He didn't know if he could stand being here for even a month. Already he was climbing the walls.

He had thought about asking his latest companion, Yvette, to come and bring her friends, and knew she would be here in an instant. But he couldn't do that because then she would read more into his invitation than he meant. Like the other women he'd been with over the years, her hints about settling down weren't so subtle and the last thing Valentino could imagine doing was giving up his freedom.

His thoughts jumped to his father, who'd been married twice. Though divorced from his first wife, he would probably still be with Valentino's mother if she were alive. Valentino wasn't like him. He enjoyed taking risks, but not when it came to women.

Though he knew nothing about his birthfather, he suspected that, since he hadn't shown a fathering instinct where Valentino had been concerned, he'd probably never married either.

At a totally loose end, Valentino headed to the kitchen for a beer. He phoned Roger, his longtime friend at the track. They talked shop for half an hour, then he checked in with Claude, the manager of his bike company in Monaco. Following that, he took a hot shower and got ready for bed.

To his irritation, his scattered thoughts returned to Clara. Throughout his years growing up in Monta Correnti, she'd been the only female constant besides his sister. He couldn't help but wonder how close she was to settling down. For the hell of it, maybe he'd take the time to find out tomorrow.

CHAPTER TWO

WHILE Clara was getting dressed in jeans and a pink cotton top with three-quarter sleeves, Bianca, who was barely pregnant again, walked in the bedroom carrying her six-month-old boy. "Mamma wants to know how you're feeling this morning."

"I'm fine," Clara murmured as she slipped into her sandals. "How's my little Paolito today?" The little boy was old enough now that when she gave him kisses on his tummy, he laughed out loud. "Do you have any idea how much I love you?" She kissed his tender neck.

"He loves his *zia* more."

Together they walked down the hall of the small stone farmhouse to the kitchen where the family ate all their meals. It used to bulge at the seams, but these days it was home to Clara, her parents and grandmother on her mother's side who lived on the main floor. Because of a stroke, the ninety-one-year-old woman was in a wheelchair. Bianca and Silvio lived upstairs with their spouses and children.

The other married siblings and extended family lived in homes on the outskirts of Monta Correnti. Now when they gathered for meals three times a day, there were only twelve at their noisy table.

Her father cast her an anxious glance. "Ah, good. You're up."

Clara kissed him on top of his balding head. "I'm up and hungry." She turned to her mother, who waited on everyone. "I'll get my own breakfast. Sit down, Mamma. You work too hard."

"No, no. You must preserve your strength."

"I have plenty of strength this morning."

"That's good to hear. Now you sit and eat!"

"Yes, *Mamacita*." She took her place across from Silvio, smiling secretly at his three children aged seven, five and three who giggled to hear their *nonna* get mad at her.

Silvio's pregnant wife, Maria, darted her a friendly glance. "You look better this morning."

"I feel good enough to run the stand today." She drank the freshly squeezed orange juice waiting for her.

"Absolutely not!" Silvio barked, so overprotective of her these days she felt smothered.

"Do you think you should?" her anxious mother questioned as she put the hot omelet in front of her. Her devoted mother who did the work of a dozen people went out of her way to make certain she was well fed.

"Of course I do. Thank you, Mamma."

"Are you telling us the truth?"

"If I weren't, I would stay in bed." Clara was getting desperate and wanted to scream, but only because everyone was so good to her and worried about her continually. More than anything she hated being a burden, yet within the last three months that was what she'd become to her hard-working family.

"So you really feel up to it?" Her father stared hard at her.

"*Sì*, Papa," she answered in a controlled voice. "Some days I wake up feeling worse than others. Right now I feel good and want to do my part around here on the days when I can."

His eyes grew suspiciously bright before he nodded. "Then it's settled."

Grazie, she murmured inwardly, but Silvio set his mug of

coffee down too hard, telling everyone his opinion. He was the sibling who stifled her most with his concern. As a result, he was the most difficult member of the family to be around.

The hot liquid splashed on the table. Maria told seven-year-old Pasquale to run and get a cloth for his father. While the mess was getting cleaned up, Bianca's husband, Tomaso, walked in the back door in his overalls. He'd been out early setting up the fruit stand for Clara before doing his own work.

His gaze shot straight to Clara. "You've got a visitor." By his awestruck countenance, it told her this was no ordinary person.

"Who is it?" She struggled to keep herself calm, already anticipating the answer with far too much excitement.

"Valentino Casali. He's driving the latest Ferrari 599."

Amidst the audible gasps, Silvio jumped to his feet, letting go with a few colorful expletives their household hadn't heard in a long time.

"*Basta*!" their father admonished him.

"Clara hasn't had anything to do with him in years, Papa. He's no good and he's not welcome on our farm. I don't want him here!" Silvio muttered angrily.

Aghast at her brother's venom, Clara felt a sudden feeling of weakness attack her body, but she fought not to show any vulnerability. She'd thought of course Valentino had only come to Monta Correnti for a few days and might even have left Italy as early as this morning.

In all the years growing up, he'd never once come to the farmhouse to see her for any reason. Every time he'd given her a ride home on the scooter on his way to the lake, she'd insisted on getting off once they reached the road leading into the farm.

"I'll go outside and see what he wants." Out of necessity she'd brushed him off too abruptly at the bus stop yesterday. Since then she'd been suffering guilt…and also regret for missing out on spending more time with him. There was no one like him! Because she'd teased him about not visiting her once in the last nine years, he'd probably decided to stop and say goodbye on his way out of town.

While everyone was reeling from the shock of their home-town celebrity showing up here, she rose from the table and walked out the back door. After rounding the corner of the house she spied the black super-car parked further down the drive.

Valentino levered himself from the front seat and strolled toward her, wearing bone-colored chinos and a black, open-necked sport shirt. He looked so fantastic she could hardly swallow. His sensuous mouth curved into a half-smile. "*Buon giorno*, Clarissima! Forgive me for coming by this early?"

Her assumption had been right. He *was* on the verge of leaving.

His eyes lingered on her soft curves before scrutinizing her from her sandaled feet to the roots of her hair. It didn't surprise her. Three years ago she and Bianca had finally taken off the weight that had plagued them most of their lives.

The diet plan she'd chosen had been part of an article by a film star featured in a celebrity magazine with a photograph of her and Valentino on the front cover. A section had been dedicated to the woman who had claimed to stay thin on the pre-scribed regimen and swore by it. Naturally there were no pictures of fat girls inside the pages of that magazine or any others.

For some reason seeing Valentino smiling at the slender beauty who'd kept her weight off had annoyed Clara. Out of anger she had started dieting and Bianca had joined her. Once they began to see results, they became local wonders for a while, but now everyone was used to the way they looked, except for Valentino, of course.

"There's nothing to forgive. You know we're a farming family, up with the sun."

His expression sobered. "I could have called your house, but thought I might have more luck talking to you if I came in person."

She was so glad he did. No doubt he was remembering how Silvio used to run interference and decided not to take the chance of her brother answering the phone. It was a good thing. Silvio's jealousy of Valentino had been over the top then. If he should see him now…

"Your car gave Tomaso a big thrill."

"But not you?" He sounded intense again, as he had yesterday.

"Of course it does!"

"It's the only transportation I have at the moment," he murmured in a voice deeper than she remembered. The eighteen-year-old Tino had become an incredibly attractive male. "Come for a drive with me. I need to talk to you."

With that silken tone, Valentino had a way of getting under her skin, but the last thing she wanted was for him to know about what was going on in her life. To spend any time with him when he was no doubt leaving town again would be like standing too near a white-hot conflagration. No more pain…

She shook her head. "I'm afraid I don't have the time. When you drove in, you saw Tomaso opening up the stand for business. I'm running it today."

"Give me five minutes."

Clara got this suffocating feeling in her chest. "Can't we talk right here?"

His striking features darkened with lines. "What are you afraid of?"

The blood hammered in her ears. She backed away from him. "Nothing! I just can't imagine what's so important you would come all this way. It's been years."

"Nine, to be exact. That's too many between old friends. I'm here to atone for my sins." His lips smiled, but for a brief moment his dark eyes looked haunted. "Surely you wouldn't refuse me as easily as you did yesterday when I offered to drive you home—"

"The bus was there. I saw no reason to put you out, but I meant no offense," she added to appease him.

"None was taken." He cocked his head. "Since you're busy now, I'll come by later in the day when you're ready to close up the stand."

Later in the day? "Please don't—" she cried, working up to a panic. After a full day's work, she would need to rest and he'd know something was wrong.

His dark brows lifted. "Have you already made plans for this evening? With a boyfriend, perhaps?"

"Yes." She leaped at the excuse he'd just given her.

Since her weight loss she'd been besieged by different guys from the valley wanting to go out with her. She'd had a lot of dates. One of the guys, Leandro, had been fairly relentless trying to get her to go out with him. When she did, she realized she had no interest in him. But Valentino didn't know any of her dating history and she wanted to keep it that way.

"What time will he be picking you up?"

"When he gets off work," she improvised.

"So when will you close the stand?"

"I—I don't know," she stammered.

"You don't know?" he enquired smoothly. "Four o'clock? Five?"

"Why are you asking me all these questions?" she blurted before realizing she'd displayed her anger. Since Valentino had never witnessed this side of her nature, he stared at her as if she'd turned into a complete stranger. In a way she *had*. Right now her heart was thudding so hard she felt ill.

"I was hoping you'd find a few minutes in your busy schedule for me." To his credit he held onto his temper.

She averted her eyes. "I'm afraid I don't have any time today," she said in a subdued tone.

"I can hear Silvio in your voice," his voice grated. "Forgive me for coming here and disturbing you. That's the last thing I wanted to do." He turned away and headed for his car.

After he'd mentioned her brother's name, she couldn't allow him to think what he was thinking. "How long are you going to be in Monta Correnti?"

He opened the car door. "For as long as it takes."

"What do you mean?"

"My father's not well."

She swallowed hard. "I'm sorry. Is it serious?"

"I hope not." He started to get in the car.

"Wait—" she called out before she realized how anxious she sounded.

His dark head reared back. "Yes?"

"I'm going into town in the morning to do some errands. If you want, I'll meet you at the Pasticceria Bonelli in the Piazza Gaspare where I caught the bus. We could have a cup of coffee or something beforehand."

"What time?"

"Shall we say ten o'clock?"

"I'll be there. *Grazie, piccola.*"

At eight the next morning Valentino dressed in a polo shirt and jeans before leaving the villa to walk to the restaurant. He entered through the back door into the kitchen with the key Isabella had given him. His plan was to eat breakfast with his father so they could talk business.

Valentino didn't hold out much hope of getting anywhere with him. His father knew the restaurant business inside and out. You couldn't tell him how to run it. Valentino could only try to make a suggestion, but even then his parent would probably resent it.

At first he didn't think anyone was about, but as he passed by the storage area that served as a pantry of sorts he glimpsed someone through the door that stood ajar. On closer inspection he realized it was his father up on a small stepladder with a clipboard. Valentino noticed his cane resting against the leg of the ladder.

Not wanting to startle him by calling out, he moved over slowly to where his father stood, but when the older man saw him, he still jumped and almost fell off the ladder. Valentino rushed to steady him. He was thinner than the last time he'd seen him just a month ago, but he still had a full head of brown hair though it was streaked with silver.

"Why did you sneak up on me like that?"

What a great beginning! Valentino had to tamp down his temper. "I was afraid if I announced myself in the doorway, you'd turn suddenly and fall. I can see you're doing the inventory. Don't you think—?"

"Not you, too—" his father barked, interrupting him. "Go on—say it! Everyone else does. Your aunt Lisa yelled at me the other day that I'm too old and crippled to run my own restaurant. That's the only reason you came back to Monta Correnti, isn't it? Isabella probably sent you in here to stop me!"

Valentino winced. His father didn't want him here. What else was new? "I haven't seen Isabella today. Isn't she at market?"

"Who knows?"

That was a lie, of course. His father knew everything. "Actually I came early so I could help you do whatever needed doing. Inventory is the only thing I'm good at when it comes to running the restaurant."

Valentino had thought he could broach his ideas for promoting Rosa while they worked together, but that was what he got for thinking. Clearly it was too soon to offer Luca anything, let alone money. His father had way too much pride for that and would throw it all back in his face.

Coming home had been a big mistake. Valentino was the last person his father wanted anything to do with. "Why don't you take a break and have breakfast with me?"

"I can't stop now."

That was clear enough. "Is there anything I can do for you today?"

"No, no. You run along and have a good time."

With those words Valentino felt about five years old. All that was missing was a pat on the head. "Then I'll see you later."

As he reached the doorway his father said, "How long will you be in town?"

The temptation to tell him he was leaving right now and wouldn't be back got stuck in his throat. "Long enough to help you. *Ciao*, Papa."

Though Valentino had been a grown man for quite some time, Luca had the power to make him feel small and unnecessary. He left the restaurant and headed through town to the piazza to wait for Clara. He wanted to be here ahead of her, in case she came early.

During their conversation he'd purposely brought up Silvio's name, knowing she'd always defended Valentino to her brother in the past. His gambit had worked enough for her to feel guilty and agree to meet him.

After ordering a cup of coffee in the pastry shop, he took it to one of the tables outside and drank it while he watched for her. At twenty to ten, Clara got off the bus.

He took a second to study her womanly figure encased in hip-hugging denim capris. She wore a three-quarter-sleeve blouse in a yellow and orange print that buttoned down the front and tied at her waist. The knockout picture she made caused male heads to turn in her direction.

Without doing anything, she elicited wolf whistles and remarks from the drivers in the heavy morning traffic circulating around the piazza, but she appeared oblivious to the attention.

He put the mug down on the table and started toward her. "Looking for someone, *signorina*?" he asked in a quiet voice.

She heard him and turned her head in his direction. Obviously she hadn't been expecting him yet.

A tiny cry escaped her throat. "Tino—" Her green eyes played over him.

Good. In that unguarded moment she hadn't forgotten after all. His lips twitched. "Do I dare confess you look good enough to eat this morning?" His comment caused color to seep into her pale cheeks. "Come inside with me. There's a *torta setteveli* with our names on it." She could do with gaining a few more pounds.

"Oh, no, not mine," she said with the infectious laugh he remembered. It made him want to provoke that response from her as often as possible. "Those days are over."

Valentino hoped not. She'd always been so happy before, but he decided not to push it. After they walked in, the woman at the counter smiled at them. "What can I get for you?"

"A large slice of that." He pointed to the *torta*. "Put it on a plate with two forks, and we'd like two cappuccinos, *per favore*."

They always used to drink it together. When she didn't demur, he assumed she still liked it.

"*Bene, signore*."

After pulling some Euros out his wallet to pay the check, he cupped Clara's elbow and steered her toward a table for two in the corner away from the window. "We'll hide over here."

"From the paparazzi, you mean?"

"From Leandro Romaggio actually. Is he the jealous type?"

She looked stunned. "How did you hear about him?"

"Restaurant gossip. You can't avoid it. Would he mind?"

Once they were seated across from each other she said, "If he knew I were here with you, he'd ask me to get your autograph. You're so famous you've become a household word in Italy."

For some reason her comment irritated him. "Does my supposed fame impress you?"

"Of course. It makes me a little sad for you, too."

His brows met. "Why do you say that?"

"Because you were always such a private person. It's quite ironic what's happened to you when I know how much you hate to be recognized everywhere you go. I honestly don't know how you've dealt with it for this long."

Her comment pleased him in ways she couldn't imagine. "Perhaps now you understand why I wanted to see you again. While the rest of the world makes the wrong assumptions about me, you alone know the real truth."

She flashed him a wistful, yet beguiling smile. "You used to complain on a regular basis that you always minded your own business, so why didn't everyone else mind theirs instead of yours!"

A chuckle came out of him. "That doesn't sound so good. I must have been pretty impossible to be around."

"Not at all. You were your own person who spoke the truth. I liked that as much as I enjoyed watching the genius at work."

"Genius—" he scoffed as the woman placed their order on the table.

"Don't be modest, Tino," she said after they were alone again. "All those drawings and experiments you did on that scooter made your fortune. A lot of the guys were jealous of you, my brother among them." She paused. "He was the reason you never stepped on our farm, wasn't he? Mamma always wondered why you stayed away."

"I didn't want him to get upset with you because of me."

"Papa told him to watch over Bianca and me. I'm afraid he took his job a little too seriously."

He took a deep breath. "That's all in the past. I'm sure Silvio does very well for himself these days."

"I'll admit he's a great help to Papa. Out of my three brothers *he* will be the one to take over the farm one day."

"Unlike me," he muttered. "I just came from being with my

father. When I offered to do the inventory with him, he told me to run along. I'm a no-account in his eyes."

"You've been away a long time. He's probably so thrilled to see you, he's terrified you'll leave again if he says something you don't like."

Her observation surprised him. "You think?"

"I know."

She said it with such authority he almost believed her. "In his eyes I'm not the dependable type, not like Silvio."

"You've already proven you can be whatever you make up your mind to be." She studied him thoughtfully. "If you're here to help your father, just give it a little time and he'll start to believe it."

Maybe she spoke the truth, but right now Valentino didn't want to talk about his father or her brother, who'd given them both grief growing up. He pushed the *torta* toward her. "The cake of the seven veils. Why don't you eat the top layer, I'll start at the bottom and we'll meet somewhere in the middle." He handed her a fork.

With a mysterious smile, she took it from him. "Maybe one bite."

While she toyed with a couple of mouthfuls, he didn't waste any time making inroads. After swallowing some of the hot liquid he said, "So that's the secret behind your weight loss."

A little chocolate remained at the corner of her pliant mouth, tempting him to taste both. The errant thought took him by surprise. Before he could blink she wiped it away with her napkin.

"The Rossettis have always been a hefty bunch. Three years ago I saw a diet plan in a magazine and decided to try it. Bianca had just gotten married and she went on it with me."

"Does she have an hourglass figure, too?"

Again he watched the blush fill her cheeks. "She looks good. Now she's pregnant again."

"Bianca has a baby?"

"Yes. Little Paolito. He's so sweet. I wish he were mine."

The throb in her voice didn't escape him. "How old is he?"

"Six months."

So much had gone on while he'd been pursuing his dreams. "So tell me what you got up to after I left Monta Correnti."

"You mean besides running the fruit stand?"

"Anything you want to divulge."

She studied him for a minute. "Do you remember Lia?"

"Of course. She was your favorite cousin who had a little white fox terrier named Horatio."

"Yes. I'm afraid he finally died of old age. Anyway, she met a man from Naples who has his own construction company. They got married five years ago and live there with their two children. Last year she begged me to come and stay with them.

"I accepted her invitation thinking I'd only be gone from the farm two weeks. Instead I got a job in his office and started business classes at college."

His dark brows lifted in surprise. "Business? What aspect of business were you thinking of going into? You told me you would never leave the farm." He'd thought he knew all of her dreams.

"The inspiration didn't come into my mind until after you left for Monaco."

"Which meant I stunted your growth."

"Don't be silly." Though she broke into gentle laughter of denial, Valentino realized he really didn't know all there was to know about her at all. That bothered him. In the past he'd taken everything about her for granted. For the first time it hit him what a shallow man he'd been. That bothered him even more.

"You've got me intrigued." Mystified was more like it.

"As you know, I spent my life in our lemon groves. One day I got this idea for doing something with lemons besides selling them."

"But not lemon furniture polish since it had already been invented, right?"

More laughter rumbled out of Clara. "Actually I came up with my own recipe for limoncello."

"Limoncello—?" In his opinion her mother was the best cook on the planet, so he probably shouldn't have been surprised. Again it showed him he'd been so consumed by his own thoughts and interests back then, he hadn't taken the time to explore hers. "Is it good?"

"My business teacher thought it was the best aperitif he'd ever tasted. He urged me to work up a model for its manufacture and distribution to present in class."

Valentino felt a sudden onset of adrenalin. "I'm jealous he got to sample it first. When am I going to taste it?"

"There's some left at Lia's, I think. I'll phone her and ask her to bring it when she comes for a relative's party tomorrow. You're welcome to try it."

"I'm going to hold you to that offer. So tell me how your project went?"

"I'm afraid I can't," she said, glancing at her watch. "I'm behind schedule now and have to go."

He stifled a protest of exasperation. Just when he was enjoying this conversation more than anything else he'd done in years, Clara was running off again. Her announcement was unacceptable to him. "Where are you going?"

"Shopping." She took one more bite of *torta*, then drank the last of her coffee.

"I'll come with you. I need to pick up a few things myself."

She laughed and shook her head. "I'm afraid this is an expedition for women only. You stay and finish the *torta*." She stood up. "It's been wonderful talking to you again, reminiscing. Thank you for the treat."

Valentino couldn't believe she was ready to leave so fast.

"Why don't we meet up later and I'll drive you back to the farm?" He got to his feet.

"That's a very generous offer, but I've made other arrangements. Now I really do have to run."

To Leandro?

He walked her to the entrance, knowing better than to try to detain her. "Thank you for meeting me, Clara. It meant a lot. I'll be in touch."

She darted him a breezy smile. "That would be lovely."

His body tautened. That would be *lovely*? Clara, Clara. What's going on with you? "*Ciao, piccola.*"

"*Ciao!*"

Frustrated by her hurried departure, he watched her progress. She had an enticing little walk that fascinated him before she disappeared around the corner. Once she was out of sight he took off in the other direction for the villa.

His father had dismissed him, and the too brief interlude with Clara had knocked him off balance. He needed to get out of Monta Correnti in the Ferrari. Opening it up always cleared his head. Why not strike out for Naples?

He could look up some old sailing buddies and visit a few tour operators to drum up business for his father. Some entrepreneur he was when he *knew* better than to approach Luca before he had something concrete to present.

The change in Clara since their first meeting must have affected him more than he'd realized, or else he was losing his edge. *Diavolo!*

CHAPTER THREE

BEFORE breakfast was over Bianca had asked Clara if she wanted help at the stand, but Clara had turned her down. Her sister suffered from bad morning sickness and helped with their grandmother and took care of Paolito while their mother did the cooking and the dishes. Her sister-in-law Maria did the house-cleaning. Everyone had their chores. Clara liked running the stand.

Their farm did big business with outlets all over the region. Trucks came and went from as far as Naples and Rome. As for the fruit stand, it existed for locals and the occasional tourist wanting a small amount of the spillover fruits or olives they could take with them in a bag. The daily intake of money from the sold produce bought the family's groceries.

After dressing in jeans and a filmy light-orange blouse with a ruffled neckline and three-quarter sleeves, Clara went to the kitchen. On the days she worked at the fruit stand, her mother always packed her a lunch.

Once she'd grabbed it and a bottle of water from the fridge, she headed out of the farmhouse. There were only a few wispy clouds above. The air was soft, just the right temperature so she wouldn't overheat while she waited on customers.

Clara felt brighter than usual today. She could attribute her energized condition to Valentino, who'd made yesterday morning magical for her. He would hate it if she told him he'd been like Cinderella's fairy godmother, transforming her life for that hour they'd spent together. It had been liberating to be treated like a normal person.

With her thoughts so full of him, she didn't realize it was Silvio, not Tomaso, who'd done the setting up with the produce from his truck and was waiting for her at the stand.

That was why he'd left the breakfast table early. Now that they were alone, she braced herself for what she sensed was coming. The knowledge cast a shadow on the beauty of the morning.

His dark eyes squinted at her. "I heard you were at the *pasticceria* with Valentino yesterday morning. Signora Bonelli's son was in the back working and saw you."

"So?"

After a sustained pause, "You shouldn't be letting that scum hang around you."

She took a deep breath. "Don't talk that way about Valentino to me. You know nothing about him. Furthermore, you don't have the right."

His scowl grew more pronounced. "You spent your whole life being his shadow. When he went away, he never gave you another thought. Now that he's back and has seen how beautiful you are, he's decided to make you his next conquest before he leaves town again."

Clara rubbed her temples with her fingers, feeling the beginnings of a headache coming on. If she put herself in her brother's place, she could understand where he was coming from except for one reason. "We're friends, Silvio. He doesn't feel that way about me, nor I him." Valentino doesn't try to protect me.

Silvio's face looked like thunder. "A man like him is capable of using a woman whether he has feelings for her or not. It infuriates me that he has suddenly shown up and taken over like he used to do."

"What do you mean take over? We were close friends all the years we were growing up. Is it so terrible that he wants to see me and catch up while he's in town?"

"What about Leandro?"

"What about him? I wasn't interested in him after our first date."

His features grew hard. "No one wants you to find love more than I do, but we're talking about Valentino Casali, who isn't capable of it, Clara. You realize it's all over the media that he's been living with that French actress."

"I know, but while he's here to see his father, he has decided to take time to renew some old friendships. We met on the staircase near the Piazza Gaspare by accident the other day. You make this sound so sinister when it's nothing like that."

Her brother wasn't listening. "You're risking your happiness to be with him again. Are you out of your mind to let him come around you?"

"If I am, it's *my* business."

"Clara—" he cried, and put his hands on her shoulders, suddenly contrite. "I didn't mean that the way it sounded."

"I know you didn't." Silvio's heart was in the right place, but he'd forgotten she wasn't a child he could order around anymore.

"Don't you know I'd do anything for you? I love you. That's why I don't want to see Valentino take you for a ride and then dump you like he's done all the other women in his life."

She eased away from him. Valentino had never shown her anything but friendship. But the implication that her brother had only ever thought of her as someone to be exploited by him, rather than be considered a lover, carried its own cruel sting.

To her relief a car pulled up the to the covered stand, preventing further conversation. It was a former customer who got into a lively conversation with her. By the time the man drove away again, Silvio had already taken off in his truck for another part of the farm. Much as she loved her brother, she was glad he'd been forced to get back to work.

For the next five hours business was fairly brisk. Clara sat at the small wooden table with the cash box and ate lunch while she waited for more customers. She'd brought a mystery book to read, but the conversation with Silvio had shaken her and she realized her mind was too focused on Valentino to get into it.

Around two-thirty she saw an old blue half-ton pickup truck coming closer. It lumbered up to the stand. The gears ground before it pulled to a stop. She got to her feet.

"*Buon giorno, signore!*" she called to the man in the straw hat and sunglasses climbing out of the cab. With his burgundy T-shirt and jeans covering his well-honed physique, she thought he looked familiar.

"It *is* a good afternoon now that I've arrived and see you standing there."

That voice—like running velvet over gravel. "*Tino*—"

"I guess my disguise isn't so bad."

She laughed so hard she almost cried. He threw his head back and laughed with her. Only Valentino would come up with something so completely outrageous. Beneath the brim, his sensual mouth had broken into a heart-stopping smile she couldn't help but reciprocate.

Everyone else wrapped her in cotton wool, but not Valentino. He was such an original and so charismatic, her heart took flight around him. Right now it was racing too fast and made her slightly dizzy. "Until you got out, the old truck and the kind of hat my grandfather used to wear had me completely fooled."

"Then it's possible I've eluded the usual horde of paparazzi."

Before she could countenance it, he went around to open the truck's tailgate. The next thing she knew he'd produced about twenty new bushel-sized baskets that he stacked near the table.

"Is this all that's left of today's produce?" He motioned to the few remaining baskets of fruits and olives.

"Yes."

Without saying anything else he loaded them in the back of his truck and shut the tailgate. Then he pulled out his wallet and put some bills in the cash box. They represented double the amount she would have received if she'd sold everything by the end of the day.

"Don't worry," he said, reading the question in her eyes. "The produce I've purchased won't go to waste."

She shook her head in amusement. "What are you up to?" The sunglasses hid a lot from view.

"What do you think? I intend to spend the rest of the day with you. Now that you've been bought out, you're free to take the time off and enjoy yourself. *Vieni com me*! I'll drive you up to the house so you can take the money inside, then we'll go." He opened the passenger door.

He'd put her in a position where she could hardly refuse. In truth she didn't want to no matter how tired she was already, no matter how loudly Silvio's warnings rang in her ears. "Will the truck make it that far?" she baited him.

His dark brows lifted. Under that hat he looked devastatingly handsome. "Shall we find out?" He helped her inside, then handed her the box after he'd climbed behind the wheel.

"Where did you get this truck?"

"From Giorgio, the sous chef at the restaurant. He has agreed to let me borrow it for a while. I've given him the use of my Ferrari whenever he wants."

"That's a trade he'll never forget, but he'll probably be terrified to drive it."

"You don't know Giorgio. Before the day is out we'll probably see him whizzing around the countryside racking up speeding tickets."

She laughed. "No doubt with the press hounds in hot pursuit."

"Exactly." He drove them up to the farmhouse, then handed her the metal box after she got out.

"I'll take this inside, then I'll be back."

"There's no hurry. I'm planning to feed you after we get to our destination."

"That sounds exciting, but I hope it's not too far. This evening I have plans I can't break." It was the truth. After a day's work she was too tired to do anything but rest. "I'll need to be home by five-thirty at the latest."

"Message received," he muttered.

She jumped down from the cab with the money box and hurried inside the farmhouse to freshen up. Luckily her mother wasn't in the kitchen at that moment. After the run-in with Silvio, she couldn't take defending her actions to anyone else, least of all her parents, who killed themselves trying to remove the stumbling blocks from her path.

While Valentino waited for Clara, his jaw hardened in frustration because she continually kept him on a short leash. Yet the minute she emerged from the farmhouse the sight of those translucent green eyes lighting up as she smiled at him broke through his borderline anger to mesmerize him.

When she climbed in the cab, he turned his head toward her. "You're meeting Leandro later?"

She averted her eyes. "I haven't seen him for a while. For your information I'm going to watch the children while the rest of the family attends my great-uncle's birthday. It's the party Lia's coming to. None of them gets a break very often. My family wants to go early so they can get home early." She flashed him an impish smile. "Both Bianca and Maria get morning sickness at night."

It was on the tip of his tongue to suggest that, since he had nothing else to do with his evening, he'd be more than happy to help her with the children. However, he thought the better of it when he remembered that, besides Paolito, the other three were Silvio's offspring. Clara's brother would probably explode in a fine fury to discover Valentino in the house. That in turn would place Clara in hot water.

"I had something else in mind for us, but under the circumstances I'll drive us to the Trattoria Alberto. They're supposed to give quick service."

"That's the place where a lot of tour buses stop. It's not too far from here. I haven't been there in years." She sounded so relieved he wondered what in blazes was going on with her.

He started up the truck and they left the farm. "How would you like to play spy?"

A chuckle escaped her throat reminding him of the old Clara. "At the trattoria?"

"Yes. One of the reasons I'm in Monta Correnti for the summer is to see what I can do to help improve business at Rosa."

"You're here for the whole summer?" The shock in her voice wasn't feigned.

"Your comment yesterday decided me."

"What comment?"

"That it will take time to get anywhere with my father." He could also see that he was going to need that much time to get back in Clara's good graces. Nine years away without checking in had done its fair share of damage.

"But what about your bike business and your racing?"

He shrugged his shoulders. "I can run it with my laptop and phone calls. Missing a few races is of little consequence right now. Papa is heavily in debt. Something needs to be done before he plunges any further. Isabella's doing her best. I need to do my part."

A hand went to her throat. "I had no idea."

"Yesterday I met with some tour operators who gave me their itineraries. They all stop at the Trattoria Alberto when they pass through Monta Correnti. I'd like to find out why they think it's a better place than Rosa. While we're eating, let's make a list of what's good and bad about the place and the food. We'll check prices and the number of menu items."

Her face lit up. "This is going to be fun."

Valentino laughed in pure delight to see her act excited. "I thought it might appeal to you."

It didn't take long before they reached the outskirts of town and pulled into the parking area at the side of the trattoria. He showed her inside and they took a seat that gave them visual access to all areas of the dining room. Without a tour-bus crowd, there were quite a few empty tables because it was still early.

Clara chose chicken and he opted for the veal, the two dishes most tourists ordered. They tested two house wines and ordered the most popular desserts. "Your father will be impressed you went to this much trouble in the name of research."

Valentino let out a caustic laugh before swallowing the last spoonful of his gelato. "To tell you the truth, his opinion of me is so low, I doubt he'll give me the time of day to present my findings, but I have to try. He raised me, after all."

She looked at him in seeming consternation. "Why do you say that? What father wouldn't be the proudest man in the world to have a son who has accomplished so much?"

"You'd be surprised." He studied her through shuttered lids. "You're very sweet, Clara."

He had half a mind to unload his secrets on her, but she seemed to have run out of steam. Her eyelids fluttered like someone who was exhausted. When he saw her glance at her watch, he knew the drill. Defeated for the moment, he laid some money on the table and ushered her outside to the truck.

On the way back to the farm she tried to keep up her end of

the conversation, but the spark she'd shown earlier had fled. After he turned onto the road leading up to the farmhouse he said, "Will you have coffee with me at Bonelli's in the morning and we'll compare notes before I head to the restaurant to see my father? I'll pick you up."

"No—I mean y-you don't need to do that," she stammered before opening the door. "I'll come on the bus, but it will have to be early, say nine o'clock. I have a dentist appointment at ten."

That was a lie. He felt it in his bones, but he couldn't prove it. "Understood. Thank you for doing this. I'm anxious for your input."

"After the delicious meal you bought me, it's my pleasure. *Domani*, Tino."

He waited until she'd entered the farmhouse. She couldn't seem to get inside fast enough. By the time he took off for Rosa, he was convinced Clara had been playing some kind of game with him from the beginning. He didn't like it. She flitted in and out of his life like a hummingbird, driving him mad.

Evidently she and Leandro weren't an item. If she were still afraid of Silvio's opinion, why risk more grief by being with Valentino at all? Her behavior raised more questions than it answered because he knew she enjoyed their time together. So did he.

All the subterfuge and time limits had to end. When he asked himself why he cared so much, the answer hit him smack in the gut. Every time you're with her, it's harder to say goodbye.

It came as a shock to discover that when we was with Clara, the thought of chucking it all in and whizzing back to Monaco held less and less appeal. This had never happened to him before.

Valentino drove in the alley at the side of the restaurant and pulled up to the back door behind the Ferrari. He got out of the truck and undid the tailgate to carry the baskets of produce into the kitchen. When he unlocked the door, Giorgio smiled at him and came out to help him bring everything inside.

"The Ferrari is sweet," he said in a low voice, kissing his fingers. "The paparazzi chased me everywhere."

"Better your picture than mine showing up in the newspaper. Many thanks for the use of your truck, Giorgio."

"My pleasure."

"I wasn't harassed once and would like to use it again sometime soon."

"No problem at all. We can make a permanent trade any time you want," he teased. "Look at the size of this!" He picked up one of the lemons. "The olives are big, too. Where did all this wonderful-looking fruit come from?"

"The Rossetti farm."

"Ah. I've heard of it. Did you sign a contract with them?"

Valentino had a hunch the type Giorgio was talking about would have to be done over Silvio's dead body. "That's up to my father. Has he been downstairs tonight?"

"No. I haven't seen him."

"What about Isabella?"

"She's out in front setting up for dinner."

"Then I won't disturb her. I'm going back to the villa. When you see her, tell her I'll be over tomorrow."

"*Bene*, Valentino."

They traded keys before he left Rosa and rocked up the mountainside in the Ferrari full of his plans for tomorrow. Clara posed an intriguing challenge, but no one loved meeting one more than Valentino.

When Clara entered the kitchen, her mother had already started cooking breakfast. She looked over at her. "Up so soon? Do you feel sick?"

"No." Just weak. She rubbed her palms against her hips in a nervous gesture.

"That's good. Your papa will be happy to hear it. He worries on these days."

"I know."

"Sit down and I'll serve you now."

"Not today, Mamma."

"But you have to eat!"

"I know. I'm having breakfast in town early."

"Are you getting together with Gina?"

"No." She hadn't talked to her friend in several weeks. "Valentino asked me to meet him at Bonelli's. He's trying to help expand his father's restaurant business."

"Why would he want to do that? It's been doing well, hasn't it?"

"Between us, his father is in debt." Her mother made a tsking sound in her throat. "We had dinner at a competitor's yesterday. This morning we're going to discuss what worked and what didn't. If he can find a way to increase tourist traffic, it will be good for his family…and him."

Clara had seen suffering in his eyes yesterday. She hadn't realized he'd had serious problems with his father. Evidently the breach between them went back years. The pain in his voice had haunted her all night.

A worried look crossed over her mother's expressive features. "Do you think it's a good idea to get this involved with Valentino?"

"We're old friends, Mamma."

"That may be true for him because you're the best friend any person could ever have and he knows it! But the difference is, you've *loved* him since the first time you met him at grade school."

"Yes, I loved him and I always will. You're confusing it with being *in love*."

"That's good you recognize the difference. You're almost twenty-eight, too old to still be nursing a dream that could never become a reality."

Clara lowered her head.

"Forgive me if that hurts you, but you see the news on television," her mother continued talking. "Valentino's been involved with that French actress lately. Last year it was a German model. Before that, an American Olympic skier." With every word that poured forth, her mother drove the nail a little deeper. "How long is he going to be in town?"

"For the summer. His father's not well."

Her mother looked shaken by the news. "Even if he stays that long, which I doubt, his home and his business are in Monaco. Eventually he'll have to go back. In the meantime you can be sure the women in his life have followed him here and won't leave him alone. Don't forget he can be with them whenever and wherever he chooses because he has the means."

"I know." *I know*.

Her mother sniffed. "If he's sandwiching you in between them for a diversion, it's only natural for him, but you're a Rossetti and Rossettis aren't content to be the crumbs off anyone else's table!"

"I agree, Mamma."

"That's good because I don't want my sweet *bambina* getting hurt in the process."

"Silvio gave me the same lecture earlier."

"Your brother feels more fiercely than the others because you grew up together. What affects you, affects him. That's how it is with twins."

Clara knew that, too. Tears streamed down her cheeks. She took a ragged breath. "When I'm with him, he treats me like we were young again, you know?" She didn't dare say she felt like an invalid around the family or it would hurt her mother.

"You think I should just tell Valentino it's time for us to let the friendship go?"

"It's not what I think—it's what you *feel* that matters!" She threw her hands in the air. "I'm just afraid you're too vulnerable right now. He wasn't voted the world's most irresistible playboy for nothing!"

She blinked. "How did you know that?"

"I happened to see it in a magazine Bianca was reading. I'm afraid your sister used to have a terrible crush on him. Do you understand what I'm trying to say? If my words sound cruel, I'm sorry because you know I love you to death."

"I love you, too," she whispered in turmoil.

"I would never say such a thing in front of the men in our family, but I say it to you. And now that I have, it is your decision what happens from here on out."

Her mother's words stayed with her while she washed the tears from her face. "I'll see you later today, Mamma." On the way out the door she grabbed an apple from the bowl to eat on the bus.

By the time she joined Valentino a half-hour later, she'd made up her mind to enjoy this morning's get-together. Maybe by the end of this day she would have gained some wisdom and would know how to tell him she couldn't see him anymore.

The problem was, he was sensitive deep down; Clara knew that and she would never want to hurt his feelings. No one would believe an insecure man lived beneath his famous persona. It stemmed from the troubled relationship with his father. He'd let her see inside him just enough for her to feel a little of his torment.

Oh, Tino.

Valentino stood at the bus stop waiting for Clara. Through his sunglasses he watched the activity in the piazza. So far his navy headscarf and striped sailor shirt with the long sleeves had disguised him enough to keep the paparazzi away.

His outfit must have done a better job than he realized because when she got off the bus at ten to nine, she walked past him in her blue print blouse and denim skirt without realizing it. He followed her into Bonelli's.

There were half a dozen people drinking coffee at individual bistro tables while they read the newspaper. He'd already staked out their table in the same corner as before.

"I'm over here, Clarissima."

She wheeled around in surprise. A slow smile broke out on her stunning face. "I would never have guessed it was you! You look like a French seaman on leave from Marseille or some such port."

"That's the way I'd like to keep it."

"I know," she said in a quiet voice. "I won't give you away."

He held her chair, then sat down opposite her. "Help yourself." He'd already taken their cappuccinos and ham-filled croissants to the table.

"Thank you. After all the food we ate last evening, can you believe I'm hungry again?" She bit into her breakfast.

Valentino smiled as he devoured his. "How did the babysitting go?"

"None of them wanted to go to bed. We ended up having our own party."

He'd wanted to be there. The night had been endless for him. "Is that why you seem a little tired this morning?"

"Yes," she murmured, but she didn't look at him as she said it.

"Did Lia bring the limoncello with her?"

Her lips curved upward. "She did."

"Good. I'm already salivating for it." Color seeped into her cheeks. "Have you given serious thought to the plus side of the trattoria?"

Clara sipped her cappuccino. "Yes. The placement of the tables was conducive to private conversation. The service was good. The chicken was tender, the gelato excellent." He liked watching her mouth as she spoke. Even when she had been a girl it had a passionate flare.

"What about the negatives?"

"The *bruschetta* was mediocre, the wine so-so, the pasta seemed too greasy and the bathroom needed attention."

He chuckled. "My sentiments exactly, *piccola*. Bravo. I was going to add that the prices were too high."

"Yes, but they obviously lower them for the tour-bus crowds. Oh—something else. The decor wasn't that unique. Not anything like your father's restaurant."

"Well, it's possible Papa will be interested in our findings and can point out the differences to the tour directors when I invite them to Rosa for a meal."

"Rosa's sauce is to die for, Tino."

"My father will be delighted to hear that Signora Rossetti's daughter has given her seal of approval. What Papa really needs is your mother in his kitchen. I ate most of your lunches at school, if you remember."

"I haven't forgotten anything," she admitted in an odd tone before suddenly getting to her feet. "Thank you for breakfast. Now I need to get going to my appointment."

For once Valentino was ready for that and stood up. "I appreciate your taking the time to meet me first." He walked her outside. "After I've met with Papa, I'll call you and tell you what he said."

As she gazed at him her eyes clouded over. "I hope he shows you how thrilled he is that his wonderful son is trying to help him." Her earnestness resonated to his insides. He couldn't hold back any longer.

"I'm not his wonderful anything, Clara. He's not my biological father. You might as well know I'm the product of an extramarital affair."

He heard her long gasp. "Your mother was unfaithful?"

"Yes. She and Luca hit a bad patch in their marriage, but they made up."

She looked devastated for him. "Do you know your birthfather?"

"No, and when I learned about it, I didn't want to know him. Neither did Luca apparently, so I was raised as a Casali."

"Then he must have loved your mother and you very much."

Valentino studied her upturned features. "You come from a very loving, close-knit family. You see only the good. It's a remarkable trait. Don't ever lose it."

She bit her lip. "You've never told anyone?"

"Isabella and Cristiano know. Our parents told all of us before Mamma died so there'd be no secrets, but it's not common knowledge."

"I'll never say anything," she whispered.

"You think I don't know that?"

"Tino—" She sounded distressed. "I—I'd like to stay longer and talk to you, but I have to go or I'll be late. Forgive me."

"Of course. I'll be in touch."

She nodded before hurrying away across the piazza. Once she disappeared he rushed after her, realizing she'd taken the set of stairs where she'd come down that first day.

When he reached it and mounted the narrow staircase to the next level of the town, she was nowhere in sight. There were more residences than shops in this area. He looked all around, noticing the local clinic on his left. He'd never known a dental office to be in there, but maybe things had changed.

Give her a few more minutes before you burst in looking for her, Casali.

If he did find her inside, he'd be risking her anger because it smacked of invading her privacy. She might never speak to him again.

After the conversation they'd had the other day on the

subject of maintaining one's privacy, there was a certain irony to this kind of thinking—and danger. But that was what he thrived on. At this late date he couldn't change his character if he tried and determined to take his chances.

He watched the locals go in and come out the doors of the clinic. He waited another minute, then walked inside. Just as he'd thought, the wall plaque didn't indicate any dentists in the building. Beyond the foyer was a waiting room full of patients. He couldn't see Clara among them. She might not be here at all, but he had to check.

Chagrined that he hadn't followed her more closely, Valentino had no choice but to approach the receptionist at the desk. When she got off the phone he said, "Could you tell me if Clara Rossetti has already gone in for her appointment?"

"I'm sorry. Even if she were a patient here, I can't give you that information unless you're the police or her next of kin."

For no good reason the hairs lifted on the back of his neck. The receptionist had given nothing away, yet for the first time since coming back to Monta Correnti a little frisson of alarm darted through him. It was that same feeling he got on the racetrack when he sensed something wasn't right and braced himself for what was coming around the next curve.

"I'm her fiancé," he lied without compunction. "I've been at sea for a long time, but got shore leave specifically to see her. Her sister Bianca told me I'd find her here for her ten o'clock appointment." If lightning struck him, he didn't care.

"In that case, go back to the foyer and down the hall to the dialysis clinic."

Dialysis—

A shudder rocked his body. That meant kidney failure. People *died* from it.

No. Not Clara. He'd just come from being with her. Though she'd looked tired, she'd seemed healthy to him.

He shook his head, trying to make sense of it.

She couldn't be dying. That was preposterous! Valentino didn't believe it. He must have misunderstood the receptionist.

Bile rose in his throat. He couldn't seem to swallow.

"*Signore*? Are you all right?" The woman at the desk stared up at him anxiously.

"Yes," he whispered.

"You didn't know?"

A groan escaped his throat. Her question made it all too real. It meant that the first day he'd seen her on the staircase between the buildings, she'd just come from the clinic.

And the other morning when she'd said she had shopping to do, she'd been on her way here...

He half staggered out to the foyer where he saw the sign for directions to the dialysis clinic.

CHAPTER FOUR

AFTER having to tear herself away from Valentino, Clara had been plunged into a new low of despair. This time it was for him.

Luca Casali wasn't his birthfather?

Though Valentino might have been living with that knowledge since childhood, a boy would still yearn to know his own flesh and blood father, or at least have *some* information about him. While Cristiano and Isabella had lived with the security of enjoying both parents' love, Valentino couldn't claim the same thing.

If Clara's life didn't depend on this treatment, she wouldn't have left him standing there in front of Bonelli's looking tortured.

Like a slot machine that went chink chink chink, little pieces of memory started fitting together in a mosaic that explained to some extent why he'd been drawn to Clara more than his own siblings during those early years. When he'd lost his mother, he'd needed a friend, no doubt because he didn't feel as if he belonged to the Casali household in quite the same way as the other two.

No one at school had had any comprehension of his struggles, including Clara. While she lay there, she wept for the boy inside the incredible man he'd become.

It was impossible to settle down and concentrate on anything else right now. Normally after she was hooked up to the large hemodialysis machine and the clinician had left the room, she could absorb herself in a good mystery novel. She'd put a new one in her purse, but hadn't opened it yet. She couldn't.

As weak as she'd felt after getting off the bus earlier today, the sight of Valentino wearing jeans that molded his powerful thighs had set off a burst of adrenalin, giving her an extra boost of energy.

He was an impossibly handsome man. In that headscarf and sailor shirt revealing his well-defined physique, he looked like a cross between a dashing pirate and a Gypsy. It couldn't be easy being so famous he had to go to such lengths to avoid the constant crush of the media.

It took a remarkable man to rise above his pain. Valentino made every moment of life exciting. That was one of his many gifts. Who else would have ordered a decadent chocolate dessert they could share and make the moment seem like a fabulous party he'd created just for her?

If Silvio knew the true Valentino the way she did, he wouldn't have grilled her so mercilessly the other morning while she'd been running the fruit stand. He'd fired questions at her she couldn't answer and wouldn't anyway.

When Valentino had come by the farm in the latest model Ferrari, it had reminded her brother of the differences between them, but that wasn't the underlying reason for his bitterness. To her dismay, the girl her brother had been infatuated with in high school had wanted nothing to do with him because she'd been so crazy about Valentino and he had gone through girls like water.

Even though Silvio had moved on to other women and had eventually married Maria, her brother's pride had never got over the rejection. As Valentino's fame grew, so did Silvio's envy for the women—the money—everything that seemed to come to him with what looked like no effort at all. In truth he couldn't forgive Valentino and didn't want Clara to have anything to do with him. In this area, he'd become irrational.

If he knew how hard it had been for Valentino growing up, even if Luca had been good to him, her brother would have a different perspective. Silvio basked in the love of both parents. All of the Rossettis did. How lucky they were!

Depleted physically and emotionally by the distressing revelation, she let out a deep sigh and closed her eyes, aching for Valentino's pain and wishing the treatments didn't take so long. But she couldn't complain, not when they were keeping her alive.

While she lay there on top of the cot fully dressed, she heard the door open. The clinician checked on her every little while. With her eyes still closed she said, "I'm doing fine, Serena."

"That's music to my ears," sounded a deep, familiar male voice.

Her eyelids flew open at the same time her heart clapped inside her chest. She discovered Valentino bigger than life, standing at the side of her bed opposite the machine. He removed his sunglasses and scarf, revealing disheveled dark brown hair. It only added to his potent male appeal.

"You *followed* me!" she cried in a combination of anger and exasperation.

"Guilty as charged."

No one had ever looked less penitent. "How did you get in here?"

"They weren't going to let me in, but I found your clinician. When I told her I was your fiancé she took pity on me."

Of course she did. Serena was a female. No woman was immune to Valentino's charm.

Clara should have been furious he'd found out her secret, but it was so like Valentino to go where angels feared to tread when he wanted answers to questions, she started to laugh and couldn't stop. Maybe it was contagious because he laughed, too. Soon the tears actually trickled from the corners of both their eyes.

They were still laughing when a smiling Serena poked her head inside the door. "I've never heard you laugh before.

There's nothing like a fiancé showing up to turn your world around, eh, Clara? I didn't know you had such a gorgeous one. You're a dark horse, you know that?"

After giving Valentino another once-over, she grinned and shut the door again. It wouldn't be long before Serena connected his looks with the legend that preceded him and would know it was all a lie. But right now Clara didn't care.

Those intelligent dark eyes of his searched hers for endless seconds. His expression grew solemn. "How long have you been undergoing these treatments, *piccola*?" he whispered in a shaky voice.

"Three weeks."

He pulled up a chair and sat down next to her with his tanned hands clasped between strong legs. She saw him looking at the graft below the place where she'd rolled up her sleeve. The loop had been surgically inserted in her right arm where her blood was drained and bathed in solution to separate the impurities before returning to her bloodstream.

She heard his sharp intake of breath. "Is this the reason you've lost so much weight?"

"No. I was perfectly healthy until two months ago when I cut my leg on one of the thorny twigs of a lemon tree at the farm. It developed into a blood infection that led to hemolytic uremic syndrome. That caused an acute failure of my kidneys."

A pulse throbbed at the corner of his hard, male mouth. "They don't function at all?"

Clara shook her head. "I have what's known as ESRD."

A bleak look entered his eyes. After a long pause, "Does this mean a kidney transplant is the only cure?" She felt his solemn tone in every sick atom of her body.

"Yes, provided it's the right match. My parents and siblings have tried to donate theirs, but because of weight problems or high blood pressure or pregnancy, they've been turned down."

He rubbed a hand over his face. "Tell me you're on a waiting list—"

"Of course."

"What kind of time are you talking here?" He fired comments and questions at her so fast she was dizzy. In fact she'd never known him to be this intense. The businessman in him had come out.

"I don't know. Waiting for a suitable match is a complicated process. You think there's one available, but then, for one reason or another, it can't or doesn't happen."

"You have a big extended family. Surely there's someone."

"Two of my relatives would be matches, but they have diabetes so that rules them out. One of my aunts was prepared to go through tests, but she has had cancer in the past and the risk is too high for her. My best chance is to receive a kidney from an altruistic donor, but they're hard to come by when thousands of people ahead of me are waiting for one."

"Tell me what you mean by altruistic."

"A non-related person who wants to give a kidney to a loved one, but it's not a match, so they still donate a kidney to someone who is. There are chains of groups of people who do this, but it's a case of finding them and linking up so their serum can be tested against my PRA."

He frowned. "PRA?"

"It means my serum has been mixed with a panel of sixty random donors to see the reaction to the antibodies. Mine is fairly low which is a plus. Kidney allocations are based on a mathematical formula. It awards points for factors that affect a successful transplant."

"What are the other factors?"

"Age and good health. I have all those things going for me."

He reached out to grasp her free hand. "How often do you come here?"

"Three times a week."

"That's virtually every other day—" He sounded aghast.

"It's not so bad when you consider there's no other way for my blood to get filtered."

"Why isn't someone in your family driving you here and picking you up?"

"I don't want to be a burden to them."

He seemed to have trouble sitting there. "You've never been a burden to anyone in your whole life."

Unbidden tears filled her eyes. "I am now. Everyone works so hard at the farm. It's bad enough that I can only do my part on the farm three days a week. There's Nonna who needs taking care of now that she's in a wheelchair and learning to talk again. Bianca has a baby and another one on the way, and Maria's expecting for the fourth time."

Valentino squeezed her fingers gently. "I've upset you when I didn't mean to. Every time we've been together, you've always had to leave. It has been so unlike the Clara I used to know, I've been at a loss. Because you didn't explain your condition to me, I had to find out the truth for myself. Forgive me for bursting in on you like this?"

His pained eyes were so imploring, she didn't want him to feel bad. After the painful experience he'd had with his father the other morning, she didn't want to add to it. "There's nothing to forgive. I didn't say anything because I've loved spending time with someone who didn't know about my condition and treated me like a normal, healthy person. If anything, I'm the one who needs to ask your forgiveness."

"*Clara…*"

She smiled at him. "You wouldn't be Tino if you hadn't made up your mind to do something no one else would think of doing to get inside this room."

"How did all this start?"

"You don't want to hear all this."

"Let me be the judge of that."

She moved her head back and forth. "Are you sure?"

Lines hardened his features. "You know me well enough to realize I never do anything I don't want to do."

Perhaps that was true once. She had no way of knowing what he was like now, but, since he showed no signs of leaving her bedside, she decided to humor him.

"After I got sick, I had to leave Lia's to come home. The doctor sent me to a specialist, who diagnosed my condition. One thing led to another and I was forced to drop out of school."

A shadow crossed over his handsome features before he found her hand again and kissed the fingertips one by one. His touch melted her like a serving of gelato left in the hot sun. "I'm going to let you rest. Before I leave, is there anything I can do for you?"

She knew it. Now that he'd learned about her condition, he was going to start treating her like all the others. In a matter of seconds she'd gone from being his fun-loving friend to invalid. He'd never held her hand and kissed it before. She couldn't bear it now. Not from him.

"Yes," she said brightly, removing it. "Will you open my purse and bring me the book I brought to read? It's on that table."

Within seconds the task was accomplished. He glanced at the title. "I've heard this is good."

"I hope so." She took it from his hand. "Thank you."

Before he left, taking all the excitement with him, he put on his sunglasses and tied the scarf around his head. "Think I'll still fool the paparazzi?" He flashed her a dazzling white smile, reminding her of the French fictional character Marius who went to sea in the story from Pagnol's *Fanny*.

At the time, she could see that Valentino totally related to the young man who dreamed of seeing the world. Clara, on the other hand, could totally relate to Fanny, who loved him, but knew she had to let him go in order for him to be happy. It was one of their favorite books in lit class. "But of course! *Au revoir*, Marius!"

Marius?

Valentino forced a grin, not having thought about that story or their involved discussions of the characters in a long time. Her humor in spite of her condition humbled him, but inside he was dying.

She looked so damned beautiful and helpless lying there, he couldn't take his eyes off her. The urge to do many things for her was so great, he needed to get out of the room in order to hold onto his sanity.

"*A presto*," he whispered, kissing her forehead.

Once he left her room, he saw Serena and headed in her direction. "Can we talk for a moment?"

"By all means."

"I lied to you before."

She smiled. "I know. If I hadn't recognized you as Valentino Casali, you would never have made it in to see Clara. The way you two were laughing in there, I knew I'd done the right thing. It's the best medicine for her."

He nodded. "Thank you for allowing me in. Would you do me one more favor and give me the name and number of her specialist?"

"Come over to the desk and I'll write it down. Dr. Arno's office is in Rome, but he's overseeing Clara's case."

Once Valentino had it in hand, he thanked her again. After leaving the clinic, he quickly found the secret alleyways through the upper region of the town, not stopping until he reached the villa.

When he checked his watch, he realized Dr. Arno would be

in his office for hours yet, that was if it were a normal day for him. No matter what, Valentino needed to talk to him.

The receptionist at his office in Rome answered. When Valentino explained the nature of his emergency, she said the doctor was on vacation and wouldn't be returning for a few more days. But she'd make certain he got back to Valentino ASAP.

Wild with pain, he needed a lot of information pronto! After hanging up, he put in a call to Dr. Rimbaud, his own doctor in Monaco, asking him to phone him back. While he waited for the call, he showered and changed into chinos and a sport shirt. He was drinking some coffee when his phone rang. Valentino grabbed for it.

"Dr. Rimbaud—thanks for getting back to me so fast."

"I thought I'd better in case you've been in another crash," he kidded him.

"Not this time."

"You sound serious, not like yourself. What's wrong?"

"Will you tell me what you can about kidney failure?"

"Uh oh. Anyone I know?"

"No. It's a close friend of mine."

"I'm sorry to hear that. Give me a few particulars."

Once Valentino had unloaded about Clara, the doctor told him what he could. "Those treatments take between four and five hours. Afterward she'll be weak and need rest. Sometimes the patient suffers a sudden loss in blood pressure or gets muscle cramps. One or all of those reasons was why she'd been in a hurry to get on the bus the other day."

"Of course." Valentino had read all the signs wrong. She'd run from him because she wasn't well, and because she had her pride. The Rossettis possessed that in abundance. Clara wouldn't even let her family drive her to the clinic and back.

"Depending on her individual health, she probably needs to eat more animal protein. If necessary she might have to cut milk, cheese, salt and soft drinks. She'll do better on the day after each dialysis treatment. That explains her ability to work at her family's fruit stand."

"How long can she go on like this?"

"Most patients live longer on dialysis these days, but her End Stage Renal Disorder might be more severe. Perhaps she's been diagnosed with anemia. There could be other problems, too, like bone disease, nerve damage or high blood pressure. These are complications you'll have to discuss with her specialist. Naturally the most desired thing would be to find a compatible donor for a transplant as soon as possible."

He closed his eyes tightly. Dr. Arno couldn't call him back fast enough. In the meantime, Valentino intended to be there for her in every conceivable way.

"Thank you, Dr. Rimbaud. What you've told me helps a lot."

"Call me anytime."

As soon as he hung up, he phoned for a taxi to take him to the local market. Once there he did some shopping, satisfied that the paparazzi would be looking in vain for his Ferrari. Until further notice it would stay in the garage. He would wait outside the doors to the clinic in the taxi until she emerged, then offer her a ride home.

"*Signore?*" the chauffeur called to him. "We've arrived."

"So we have."

He instructed him to wait in the loading zone. His pulse picked up speed when he finally saw Clara start out the clinic doors. She looked good, not as pale as she'd been last evening. He stepped out of the taxi into her path so she had to stop.

"How come you keep following me?" he baited her gently.

She lifted her beautiful head so he could see the green flecks in her eyes.

"Tino—"she cried in shock, but her eyes lit up. This was a bonus he hadn't expected after barging in on her treatment.

"Come on. I've brought cold fruit juice and a chicken sandwich for you. You can eat it on the way back to the farm."

He could tell she wanted to argue with him, but she didn't have the kind of strength she needed for that. "Where's the Ferrari?" she asked as he helped her into the backseat.

After he gave the driver directions, he handed her a sandwich and a drink before sitting back to answer her question. "It's out of sight for a variety of reasons."

"That will drive the paparazzi crazy." She took several bites of her sandwich. "I have to admit this tastes delicious. You're spoiling me with good food again."

He'd bought himself a fruit drink and drained most of it. "I wonder how many hundreds of times you shared your lunch with me at school because I was too busy doing some project to stop and eat. Your mother made the best lunches in Monta Correnti."

A trace of a smile hovered on her lips as she continued to eat. "Our family carried around the excess pounds to prove it."

He flashed her a sweeping glance. "Not any longer."

She avoided his gaze and drank more juice.

"Does your mother know she kept me alive with her cooking?"

"I didn't dare tell her."

Valentino chuckled. "You're lucky you've had her in your life all these years. Do you want to know a secret?"

Clara's head turned in his direction. She'd finished the last of her sandwich. He was thankful she'd had an appetite. "What is it?"

"I was jealous you had a mother who fussed over you every day. You and Bianca always seemed so happy. You didn't know it, but having two parents who were alive and loved you gave you a confidence I would have given anything to feel."

Her expression sobered. "I understand that now, but you did have Luca."

"Yes, and he indulged me without limits."

"That was only natural. After your mother died, he would have tried to play both roles. He loved you, Tino. I know he did. Otherwise his marriage to your mother wouldn't have worked out."

"I guess he wanted her badly enough to include her excess baggage."

In a surprise gesture she covered his hand with her own and squeezed it gently. "I'm so sorry you've carried this pain with you all these years. I often sensed something was wrong, but you never opened up about it."

"I couldn't."

Her head was bowed. "None of us is exempt from problems, but somehow we deal with them because we have no choice, right?"

He marveled at her courage. "*Sì*."

She let go of his hand. "We're almost to the farm."

Valentino told the driver to turn onto the private road where you could see the sign advertising produce at the Rossetti farm. He told him to follow it all the way in to the farmhouse and pull to a stop.

The minute the taxi slowed down, Clara had the door open. He knew better than to ask her to stay with him and talk. She was probably craving her bed.

"Thank you for the food and the ride, Tino. You saved my life today."

Would that were possible.

"I always enjoy being with you."

She couldn't meet his gaze. "Where are you going now?"

"Home to work on the Web site."

"What did your father say about your ideas?"

"I've decided to wait until I have all the facts at hand, then present them in one go and see how he reacts."

"I think you'll be surprised how accepting he is of your ideas."

"We'll see. Your optimism gives me hope."

"That's good," came her fervent reply.

He leaned toward her. "I'm going to come by for you in the truck after you're off work tomorrow."

Clara felt her pulse race. "What did you have in mind?"

"I thought we'd drive to Gaeta—we went there once, remember? We'll enjoy a meal on the coast. It's not too far. We'll take it in stages. If you feel like sleeping on the way, you can."

He still wanted to be with her?

"I'd love it!" she broke in. To go to the sea with him sounded divine.

His mouth broke into a satisfied smile. "I'm happy to hear it. Get a good sleep. I'll be by about three."

"All right. *Ciao.*"

Clara entered the kitchen feeling more light-hearted than she'd been in days. Who else but Valentino would have pretended to be her fiancé so he could gain access to the treatment room? She'd noticed that none of the workers at the clinic were immune to his compelling personality and looks. He'd been the talk of the place. Serena had been totally won over.

As for the taxi waiting for her, it might as well have been a golden coach whisking her away from the castle with her dashing prince while he fed her on the way. Because of his kindness, her body didn't get a chance to feel depleted as it did when she had to walk down to the piazza and then wait for the bus.

She'd been utterly shocked to see him outside the doors. And grateful… He could have no idea how wonderful it was to just get in the car and be waited on as if she were a princess.

Though he'd told her earlier that he had no interest in knowing the identity of the man who'd had an affair with his mother, Clara couldn't help but think his birthfather must have been an extraordinary person with exceptional looks and drive. Otherwise Valentino wouldn't have turned out to be such a brilliant entrepreneur and heartthrob.

"What's the great Valentino Casali doing bringing you home in a taxi?" Silvio had just walked in the kitchen. He wasn't usually home this early.

"He was thoughtful enough to give me a lift from town."

Her brother grimaced. "Did he think that by not bringing you in the Ferrari, the family wouldn't notice?"

"Why would he be concerned about that?" she asked, attempting to control her temper without much success. "If he didn't choose to drive it, it was probably because he was tired of the paparazzi following him every second of his life."

"Why do you let him do it?" he demanded. "Don't you get it?"

"You can stop worrying. It hardly smacks of the kind of attention you're talking about. I'm a dying woman."

"Don't ever say that again!" he cried.

"But I *am* dying, Silvio. You have to face it. We're all going to die some time. I just happen to know that without a new kidney, it will happen to me sooner than later."

"How can you talk that way?"

"How can I not? You've got to stop being angry about it. As things get worse, Mamma and Papa are going to need your strength, not your rage."

His eyes grew moist. "You've been so brave. If the almighty Casali had any idea what you're dealing with now—"

"Actually he does. In fact he sat with me in the clinic today while I was getting my treatment."

"I don't believe it," his voice shook. "You *told* him you have ESRD?"

"No. We met in town before my appointment. After I said goodbye to him, he followed me to the clinic and pretended to be…a relative." She caught herself in time. "He did that so he could get in to see me. At the end of the treatment he brought me home so I wouldn't have to take the bus. He even brought food and drinks because he knew I needed it after dialysis."

Silvio looked dumbfounded.

"Please let's not argue over him. He's been nothing but kind to me and now I'm tired." She felt his eyes on her as she left the kitchen to go upstairs. All she wanted to do was go to bed and dream about tomorrow when he came for her.

One more outing, then she'd tell him that, as much as she enjoyed his company, her illness was slowly draining her to the point that any social life had to end. She was hurtling through space toward a black void from which there could be no return. Where she was going, he couldn't go.

She knew Valentino well enough to know his compassion for her condition would prompt him to continue making himself available to her. She also knew herself well enough to know she would cling more and more to him because he *was* life to her.

Clara couldn't think of a worse scenario for a man whose freedom meant everything to him.

On the way back to town, Valentino had to admit it was getting more difficult to drive away after they'd been together. When he thought about it, he'd never liked parting company with Clara. Until he heard from the doctor, he was going to be on tenterhooks.

In the meantime he needed to keep so busy he wouldn't be able to think. But he soon discovered that work was no panacea for his heartache. Nothing could take it away. It went so deep, he couldn't find solace.

Every time he thought about her pain and what she was facing, he was pierced to the quick. His agony drove him to get in his car. He started driving through the countryside with no destination in mind. While he was en route, the wildflowers seemed to flaunt their fragrance in the night air as if to impress upon him the delights Clara might not be able to enjoy much longer.

Crazed by the thought that a life as sweet and innocent as

hers could be coming to an end, he found himself headed for the church. Eventually he pulled up in front of the rectory. It was after nine p.m. when he levered himself from the car and was made instantly aware of the sound of crickets chirping. Tonight all his senses had come alive to nature, sending bitter-sweet pains through his body.

He took the steep steps two at a time to gain the porch, not hesitating to tug on the bell pull. In a few minutes, a much younger priest he didn't recognize opened the door.

"Yes?"

"I'm here on an emergency to see Father Orsini. Is he still awake?"

"I believe so."

"Will you tell him it's Valentino Casali? If he can see me, tell him I'll be out here waiting for him."

The other man studied him for a brief moment. "*Bene*," he said before shutting the door.

Unable to remain still, Valentino walked to the wrought-iron railing and looked out over Monta Correnti. The lights of the town with its red-tiled roofs and centuries-old palazzos spilled over the undulating hills, creating a fairyland illusion. In the distance, the Rossetti farm made up part of the magical landscape.

Would that what he'd learned at the clinic today were just a bad dream from which he'd awaken at any moment.

"Valentino?" came a familiar voice. "Don't tell me you're here to confess ten years' worth of sins?" He'd asked the question in a joking manner, but the ring of hope lingered in the night air.

Consumed by a guilt so deep he'd never been able to talk about it, he turned to face the gray-haired priest who'd grown much more frail over the last decade. "Not tonight, Father. Otherwise you would never get to bed," he teased. Their easy relationship stretched back to Valentino's childhood.

Father Orsini chuckled. The years hadn't deprived him of a sense of humor, for which Valentino was thankful. "It's good to see you."

"Then you'll understand how pleased I was when Father Bruno told me Monta Correnti's most legendary figure was outside waiting for me."

"Let's not play games, Father. A legendary figure should at least connote someone worthy." He shifted his weight. "Forgive me for calling on you so late, but this couldn't wait."

"Evidently not. Let me put it another way. What's troubling Luca Casali's most famous son?"

"Famous for what?" Valentino muttered in self-abnegation. "Certainly nothing that matters." When the priest blinked in astonishment, Valentino added, "Did Luca or my mother ever take the opportunity to tell you I'm not his birth son?"

"*What is this?*" Father Orsini cried out aghast.

"I don't blame you for being bewildered. Forget I asked."

"My son—"

"It's all right, Father. If you *did* know, you couldn't reveal it anyway. He and Mamma told me the truth years ago. It was a good idea at the time considering I don't look or behave anything like Isabella or Cristiano."

"Do your siblings know?"

"You mean that my infamous qualities can be laid at my biological father's feet?" he mocked. "Yes, but that's not why I'm here. What I'm hoping is that you'll be able to help me over another matter. It's of life and death importance."

The priest cleared his throat. "If I can, but that places a great burden on me."

Valentino squinted at him. "I knew you'd say that, but I have nowhere else to turn." He stared at the priest. "What do you know about Clara Rossetti?"

In the quiet that followed, a sadness entered Father Orsini's eyes and he pursed his lips, giving Valentino the answer. Fresh pain arced through him as surely as if he'd crashed on the track and the paramedics couldn't separate his body from the wreckage.

The compassionate priest put a hand on Valentino's shoulder. "She doesn't want to die and is fighting this with everything she has in her."

Valentino's body trembled. "I know. I've been with her every day since I came home. She's so courageous, I'm in awe of her."

"You two were very close growing up."

A sob got trapped in his throat. "Very. I don't want her to die, Father."

"Of course you don't. After being away such a long time, this news must have come as a great shock."

Shock hardly covered it. Shame for his narcissistic lifestyle had seeped into his soul. Up to now Valentino had lived only for his own pleasures. He'd avoided marriage and children in order to pursue new adventures without suffering any more guilt than he already dragged around.

In the process he'd pretty well abandoned his family, not to mention Clara. Valentino wasn't only selfish, he was a coward unwilling to face certain unpalatable truths. After his aunt Lisa had leaked the latest family secret, his first instinct had been to run away and stay in denial. That had been his pattern over the years.

That was the mortifying part. After spending time with him during their growing-up years, Clara had become so well acquainted with his self-focused obsessions, she'd written him off when he'd left in his late teens. And why not?

What had he ever done for her?

His hands curled into fists.

Nothing! Not a damn thing!

It strained his credulity that she'd given him the time of day since he'd been back. While he'd been off in his superficial world, angry at life while he tried to break barriers and set new bars, she had been battling for her life!

Somewhere in his psyche Valentino had known there'd be a price to pay for always running away, for always taking without giving anything back. He just hadn't expected it to come now, in this particular form. Clara, more than any other human being, had shown him unqualified friendship, but he hadn't realized or understood until it was too late.

"I can see you're in pain, my son."

"I want to help her, but I don't know where to begin."

"She could use a good friend."

Something he hadn't been.

"Is there anything else you'd like to discuss with me?"

Valentino shook his head. "No, *grazie*." He had quite enough on his plate and had said more than he should already. Calling on the priest this late at night constituted a special act of selfishness all its own, the kind for which Valentino was famous.

Luca's "famous" son who really wasn't his son. The negative connotation fit.

"I've intruded on your time long enough. Thank you for seeing me, Father. *Buona notte.*" He started down the stairs.

"Don't be such a stranger!" the old priest called after him.

Valentino deserved that particular distinction, too. A stranger was one who was neither a friend nor an acquaintance. Those who knew his name would say that pretty well summed up his existence.

He waved to the priest from the lowered window of the car before he headed back to the villa. His black thoughts drove him to the kitchen where he made a pot of strong coffee. On an empty stomach the caffeine was guaranteed to keep him wired for the rest of the night. He did his best thinking when he prowled around in the dark.

The priest's words wouldn't leave him alone. *She could use a good friend.*

That meant making a commitment you didn't break.

For the rest of the night Valentino searched his soul. By the time morning came eight hours later, he'd determined Clara Rossetti would discover how good a friend he could be, even if she didn't believe it right now.

CHAPTER FIVE

"VALENTINO has come for me, Mamma. We're driving to Gaeta. Just so you know, I've come to a decision. After today, I won't be seeing him anymore. He knows I'm dying, and he'll respect my wishes."

Her mother let out a heavy sigh and stopped stirring the sauce she was cooking. "I'm glad to hear it, for his sake as well as yours. And I'll tell you something else. You're not going to die if *I* can help it! The doctor has assured me they're doing everything to find the right donor for you. God hears me beg for your life every minute of the day and night."

Clara lowered her head, humbled by her mother's love. The doctor had told them they needed a miracle, but she knew that even if a kidney became available from a non-relative, there was always the possibility her body would reject it.

"See you later, Mamma." She hugged her mother, then hurried outside to the old truck. Valentino got out of the cab wearing the same straw hat. When she drew closer, he flashed her a broad smile.

"*Buon giorno, piccola.*" He was hiding something behind his back.

"What have you got there?"

"You need a disguise, too," he said before putting a matching hat on her head. "You look very fetching with it perched at that angle. From a distance we'll look like an old farming couple taking a break after a busy morning."

She loved it! They left the farm and headed in the direction of the coast. The truck made for slow going, but she felt very much at home in it. The Rossettis didn't drive anything but trucks.

They ate some plums he brought and made desultory conversation while they drove through the enchanting countryside. Clara felt so carefree and relaxed that in time she found her eyelids drooping and fought to stay awake.

Nestling against the door, she closed her eyes, telling herself it would only be for a moment. The next time she became aware of her surroundings, she was cognizant of two things: the tangy smell of the Mediterranean and the feel of Valentino's hard-muscled arm against her cheek and shoulder. He'd always smelled so good. It had to be from the soap he used in the shower.

"Oh—I'm sorry—" She sat up horribly embarrassed that she'd been asleep for an hour with her arm against him. Her hat was askew. How was it she'd ended up pressed to the side of his fit body instead of the door? Looking straight ahead, she glimpsed the Gulf of Gaeta spread out before her like a sparkling blue jewel in the sunlight.

Valentino had removed his sunglasses and cast her a sideward glance. "Why apologize? You needed your sleep. I'm hungry and presume you are, too."

"I am." Food had never sounded so good to her before.

"After we eat, we'll take a walk on the beach if it's warm enough for you and you're up to it."

Mentally she was up for everything he suggested, but her body had other ideas. Still she wouldn't think negative thoughts right now, not when this would be her last outing with him. Certainly not when they were passing through hills of rich green vegetation where she spied a fabulous pink hotel surrounded by palm trees and a fabulous garden. "I remember that place from before! Didn't you tell me it was once a monastery?"

"You have an excellent memory. It's the Villa Irlanda. I thought we'd eat by the pool where there's a view of the coast. I was in too big a hurry to stop here last time. It's an oversight I intend to correct now. When I look back on my life, I think I was always in a hurry, but no longer."

Valentino waited in the hotel lounge for Clara, who went into the ladies' room. When she came out again a few minutes later, he escorted her to the pool where they settled on loungers to soak up some sun. They had the place to themselves. He signaled one of the waiters, who came right over.

After greeting them, he named half a dozen entrees on the menu. "But may I suggest that the oven-roasted *abbacchio* with rosemary, white wine and peppers would be a superb choice. You couldn't go wrong with a side dish of *carciofi alla romana*."

"What do you think, Clara?" In the late afternoon sun her eyes glowed an impossibly iridescent green. Fringed by her long black lashes, their color mesmerized him.

"I love lamb. As for artichokes, I've never had them stuffed with mint. It all sounds delicious."

"I think so, too." He placed their order, asking that it be served with his favorite pinot noir. When the waiter walked away, Valentino turned to her. She was a totally feminine creature, one of the few who could wear a blouse with a ruffle like that. "Can you drink wine?"

"In moderation. I have to stay away from sodas."

Valentino thought she looked a little pale. No doubt her work at the fruit stand had drained her. "How are you feeling right now?"

"Good."

"Still, I can tell something's wrong. You don't have to hide anything from me."

She let out a small laugh. "Apparently I'm not able to hide anything from you. To be honest, the air's not as warm here as it was at the farm."

"If you're chilly, that's an easy fix." Valentino was relieved the temperature had turned out to be the culprit for the moment. "Come with me." He helped her to her feet and they walked back inside the hotel to the front desk.

When he told the concierge he wanted a room with a view of the sea, he could see Clara shake her head no, but he pretended not to notice. After making arrangements for dinner to be brought to their room, he escorted her upstairs to a suite with a sweeping vista of the grounds and coastline. It was definitely warmer inside.

"Tino—" She laughed as he moved the table and chairs in the corner of the room to the center of the window.

"I want a view while we eat," he declared. "In the meantime, you can lie down until our dinner comes."

"Have you forgotten I slept in the truck?" Ignoring the suggestion, she sat down on one of the chairs. "Why didn't we just eat in the restaurant?"

He could tell something was bothering her. "Because I wanted you to feel totally comfortable."

"That's very considerate, but are you sure you weren't afraid the paparazzi would sneak in and take pictures of us that will make tonight's ten o'clock news?"

He took a fortifying breath while he tried to understand her sudden burst of heated emotion. "For once the thought hadn't even crossed my mind."

"I don't think Giselle Artois would be happy about it."

Ah. Giselle… Valentino frowned. "She's engaged to her long-time British lover."

Her eyes widened. "But on the news it sa—"

"Forget the news," he cut her off. "They say and print whatever they feel like, but it has nothing to do with the truth. In all honesty there's something I have to say to you and I wanted it to be in private. The restaurant wouldn't have afforded us a moment to ourselves."

To his dismay she paled a little more. It wasn't his imagination that she was all tensed up.

"Tino? Can I speak frankly?"

"Always."

"You said you need to talk me, but there's no point in going to these elaborate lengths in order for us to be alone." More of that hidden temper of hers was showing.

"What are you getting at, *piccola*?"

She plucked at her napkin. "Since you came back to Monta Correnti, don't think I haven't appreciated everything you've done for me, but now it has to stop."

He put his hands on his hips. "Where's all this coming from?"

Before he knew it, she'd jumped to her feet. "Over the last few days you've more than made up for the nine years of silence, and I'll never forget your kindness. But we're going in different directions and I'm not unaware you have personal commitments and a business to run. Entertaining me wasn't your plan when you came here."

A knock on the door interrupted them. He'd never seen her this wound up in his life. Normally unflappable Clara had just delivered the longest impassioned speech she'd ever made, revealing another unexpected side to her nature.

"I'll get it."

One of the staff from the kitchen wheeled in a tea cart with their meal. Valentino gave him a tip, then shut the door and pushed it across the room to the table. With her beautiful body still taut, she held onto the back of one of the chairs while she stared out the window.

Intrigued by her behavior, he put everything on the table and invited her to sit down. "We need to eat our food while it's hot. I wanted this to be special for you. Earlier you admitted you were hungry."

The reminder eventually forced her to comply. Gratified to see her food start to disappear, he poured them some wine and picked up his glass. "I'd like to propose a toast."

Her fingers tightened around the stem of her wine glass as if she were barely holding onto her control and would like to crush it. After a minute she lifted the glass. "Let me go first."

"By all means," he murmured.

"To our old friendship."

He'd seen that one coming. After he touched her glass, they both drank.

"Now it's my turn." Trapping her gaze, he said, "To our new one."

The second the words were out, she looked down without drinking. He swallowed the rest of his wine while he waited for her to absorb what he'd just told her.

She pushed her glass away. "We can't have a new one. I'd like to go home now, Tino."

"Not until you've heard me out."

Her head reared back. Green sparks flew from her eyes. "I'm not trying to be intentionally rude, but I don't want to listen to anything else."

"Not even if this is vitally important to both of us?" When she didn't immediately shut him down he said, "Last night I went to see Father Orsini, but there was one thing I couldn't bring myself to confess to him."

He saw the shiver that ran through her body. "If you're thinking of telling me what you couldn't tell him because I'm dying, please don't. I'm not a priest."

His chuckle permeated to her insides. "No, you're not,

grazie a Dio. But you *are* the woman I want to marry as soon as possible."

After a long silence, he heard hurtful laughter come out of her. "Me—marry you—" she mocked in a brittle tone.

"Yes."

"It sounds like you've come to the rock bottom of your many excellent adventures. I thought you were the one person who wasn't like everyone else, but I was wrong."

Like the lash of a whip, he felt her salvo. "That's the first unkind remark you've ever made to me."

"Maybe it's because even a dying farm girl doesn't relish the idea of being the object of Valentino Casali's pity."

She got up from the table hot-faced and made a dignified exit from the room. He hurried down to the front desk to pay the bill, then raced after her. When he crossed the parking south of the hotel he found her waiting for him in the cab of the truck with her hat on.

They started back to Monta Correnti. He noticed she stayed close to the door so neither their arms or legs would brush by accident. "Pity comes in many forms, *piccola*," he began. "It depends on the point of view. I'm counting on yours to save me from myself."

Clara didn't want to listen. Valentino had a way of twisting words and meanings until he threw her into a state of confusion. Maybe she was having some strange, distorted dream where the impossible was happening and everything was out of her control.

"Before you consign me to my rightful place, which is a great deal lower than the angels, you need to know I called my doctor in Monaco. Among the things we talked about, he said I can be trained to help you do dialysis at home so you don't have to go to the clinic. They have these new machines so you can even travel with them and carry on your activities."

She couldn't imagine anything more wonderful, but not at Valentino's expense.

"Your mother can show me what kind of meals to make for you. I'm a good cook. I've had to be. The villa has a view of the town and valley from every window. Your family can visit all the time. You can visit them and still run the fruit stand if you want.

"While we're waiting for a kidney, we'll do everything together like we did when we were at school. We'll have fun. When was the last time you had fun? I know I haven't had any. I have to reach back to those years with you to remember what it was like to enjoy a carefree day. Marry me and make me respectable. I need you so much more than you need me."

Oh, Tino. The issues with his father had robbed him of so much confidence. She'd never dreamed they were this serious.

"Allow me to take care of you, *piccola*. Now that I've come home, I can't be around my family, my aunt and cousins, without your help. Since you talked to me about my father yesterday, you've made me realize I have to try harder."

She couldn't believe what she was hearing. "What about the woman in your life? I'm not talking about Giselle now."

"What woman?"

"Don't tease about this, Tino. It's too important."

"I agree. I guess it's confession time. There have been other women, but not as many as you have imagined. Even the few I had a relationship with didn't inspire me to get married. I suppose I didn't feel I could count on them for the long haul. If I'd wanted to make a lifelong commitment with one of them, I wouldn't be here now."

"Even so—"

"Even so nothing! What about the men in your life? Don't tell me there haven't been any because I wouldn't believe you."

"No. I won't tell you that, but my illness has changed everything."

"Then there's no problem."

She sucked in her breath, trying to keep her wits about her. "Of course there is! You can't just give up your racing and let your team down."

"You haven't been listening to me. Though I haven't officially announced it yet, it's over."

"Since when?"

"It's been over in my mind for quite a while. Isabella has been after me to come home, but it wasn't until I knew I wanted to marry you that the issue was finally settled for me. Our marriage needs to take place right away so we don't lose any more time. Something quiet and private that won't wear you out."

What he was saying had shaken her to the foundations.

"When we get back to the farm, I want to tell your family so we can make plans right away. The one thing they won't be able to say is that we haven't known each other long enough. From the age of seven to eighteen, I probably saw or spent time with you every day of your life, whether at school or church."

Clara stirred restlessly on the seat, trying to get her bearings. "That's true, but they're going to ask about all the years since then."

A smile hovered around his male mouth. "Surely your parents read about mine or watched it on TV. My last nine years have been lived in a fish bowl. The public seems to know more about my life than I do, but the one thing no one knows except you is my pain. It's time for the pain to end for both of us. Don't you agree?"

She knew what he was asking, but she couldn't answer him. Bands constricted her breathing. They made the rest of the trip home in silence. When he drove them straight up to the farmhouse and turned off the ignition, she started to panic.

"I need an answer, Clara." He turned to her, his eyes blazing. "If it's no, I'll still go on doing everything in my power to help you, but I'm telling you right now it won't be enough for me."

While she sat there trembling from the reasons he wanted this marriage, he got out of the truck and came around to help her down. He'd given her a choice. They could go on being friends as they used to be, always parting company at the end of the day. Or, they could be friends around the clock so he had the support he claimed he needed to be around his family and in return she would get the support she needed through her illness.

If it was an elaborate lie he'd concocted to make her feel better, she couldn't bear it. Finally she turned to him. "I'm afraid the answer has to be no, but I'll never forget your generous gesture. *Arrivederci*, Tino."

While Luca was having a bad morning and stayed upstairs, Valentino got to work and finished the inventory. It had taken him until four in the afternoon.

He found Isabella in the kitchen talking to Giorgio. "The deed is done, Izzy." He put the clipboard in her hands.

She stared at him in shock. "You're a speed demon."

"It's what happens when you're focused." He'd kept up a frantic pace so he wouldn't go crazy waiting for Clara's dialysis to be over for the day. "I would tell Papa myself, but I'll be late picking up Clara." His glance swerved to Giorgio. "Thanks for the use of the truck again."

"Anytime. You know that."

He kissed his sister's cheek and hurried out the back entrance where he'd left the Ferrari.

En route to the clinic he checked with Serena to be certain Clara hadn't left yet. To his relief she wouldn't be out for fifteen more minutes. That gave him time to pick up some food and drinks for them.

After he'd made his purchases, he parked in the loading zone and got out to watch people as they exited the clinic. Eventually he saw her emerge dressed in a yellow top and white skirt. She looked fabulous in anything, but her features were drawn and pale. To know she was so ill squeezed his heart to a pulp.

"Clara?" he called to her.

She glanced at him, then picked up her pace in order to get away from him. In a few swift strides he caught up to her and spun her around gently.

Her eyes looked tormented. "You shouldn't have come."

"I told you I'd be here for you no matter what."

Clara shook her head. "This has to stop, Tino."

"Let's argue about it in the truck. Come on. I brought food. I know you're starving and so am I after putting in a full day of work at the restaurant. You'll be pleased to know I got the inventory done for my father."

"I'm sure that made him happy."

"We'll see." He helped her into the cab, then walked around and got behind the wheel. "I thought we'd eat at the park by our old school before I take you home. It's on the way."

As they drove off she stared out the passenger window not saying anything. "Was it a bad day, *piccola*?"

"I'd rather not talk about it."

"Then we won't."

Before long they wound around to a grassy section of the park. He slowed to a stop beneath some shade trees. "I think you're too tired to get out, so we'll eat right here." He handed her a sandwich and drink from the bag sitting between them.

Her hunger won out and she ate. After they'd both finished their food he turned to her. "I didn't get to say all I needed to say to you last night."

"You said enough and I told you no."

"Five more minutes is all I ask. If your answer is still no, I won't bring it up again."

She lowered her head. "What is it?"

"I want to tell you the secret I couldn't tell Father Orsini."

"Tino—"

"It's about the details of my mother's death."

Here came his tentacle hooks, grabbing hold of Clara so she was a captive audience, but she kept telling herself she was going to wake up at any second and find herself at home in bed, or at the clinic.

"Did I ever tell you Mamma was a diabetic?"

"No." She hadn't heard that.

"She suffered from dizzy spells, a lot, and was battling a severe one the day she slipped on one of my toys and fell down the stairs. We were alone in the house. I was only five at the time and tried to get her to breathe again, but she wouldn't wake up."

Stop talking, Tino.

"I can still remember my terror because I didn't know what to do. I didn't know how to use the phone and there weren't any neighbors close by. A helplessness went through me the likes of which I'd never known. I loved her so much and re-member lying down next to her, sobbing. Cristiano was sup-posed to be home. I prayed for him to come."

You're breaking my heart.

"The second I heard him come in the house, I ran screaming to him and told him what had happened. He took one look at Mamma and called for the ambulance, but when it came, it was too late. The look he gave me made me want to shrivel up and die."

A moan escaped Clara's throat.

"Her death has plagued me all my life. I always felt the family blamed me, especially since I wasn't Papa's real son."

Her head flew back. "But you *were* his son in all the other ways that counted."

He shook his head. She still couldn't reach him on that point.

"From then on I stayed away from the house as much as

possible. You were always kind to me. You were so good and pure and you accepted me for the way I was. I found myself clinging to you."

"Oh, Tino—" Clara had had no idea of the depth of pain he'd suffered.

"I figured that one day when I was older, I would go away so no one would have to be reminded of what a terrible person I was."

"But you didn't do anything wrong!" she cried, shaking her head in despair.

"When I grew to adulthood, I gained an intellectual understanding of what had happened, but emotionally…? To make matters worse, my long absences from home did a lot of damage to the rest of the family. My aunt Lisa took great satisfaction in letting me know I'd let everyone down."

She held her head in her hands. "All this was going on inside you and you never said a word."

"I couldn't. I felt too frozen inside. Isabella kept begging me to come back and help with Papa, but I was too torn apart by my fears to do what she asked. I know Cristiano hasn't come back because deep down he still blames me and would rather not be around to be reminded of what happened."

"That couldn't possibly be true!"

"She was our mother, Clara. He adored her, too. I should have done something—I should have been able to find a way to get help—"

She couldn't stand to hear him go on like this. The torment in his voice was too much. His features were etched in the kind of pain and deep-seated sorrow she wished she could take away.

"Let me ask you a question, Tino. If it had been Cristiano instead of you who was home that day, would you still be blaming him?"

He took a fortifying breath. "You already know the answer to that. He was older and could have prevented her death."

"How do you know she didn't die on impact? If that's the case, then no one could have saved her. Did you ever see the coroner's report?"

Valentino stared at her as if he'd never seen her before. "No," he whispered.

"Then I suggest you ask to see it before you go on crucifying yourself."

Before she could countenance it, he grasped the hand closest to him. "You see how much I need you? How good you are?" He squeezed her hand tighter. "There's only one reason I told you about Mamma's accident. When I saw you lying there getting a treatment the other day, that same feeling of helplessness and despair swept over me. Do you know why?"

She shook her head.

"Because *you* are part of that part of my life, Clara."

"I—I don't understand." Her voice faltered.

"In my mind I can't separate you and our memories from those early years. Since we met again in town and I felt you push me away, a sense of panic took hold of me until I could get to the bottom of your behavior. I swear it was like the angels had shoved me away from heaven's door."

"I'm sorry." Clara bowed her head, her emotions in utter chaos.

"Maybe what you've said is true and no one could have helped my mother stay alive. It's all in the past now anyway, but if I'm your husband, I can help *you* stay alive. I can be there night and day for you to do things no one else can do to ease your burden."

What Valentino was saying went through her like a thunderbolt.

She wasn't prepared for him to pull her into his arms. He buried his face in her hair. "Let me do for you what I couldn't do for my mother," he begged with tears in his voice. "I need to do this, Clara."

His entreaty reached down into her soul. Given the option of being with him all the time, there was no other choice for her, not now that he'd opened up all of his soul to her. He was tortured by his mother's death and the guilt that went with it, but then her soul was tortured, too.

She stayed in his arms for a long time. Last night she'd been so tormented, she hadn't been able to sleep. Though she'd been tempted to accept his proposal, she'd kept remembering her mother's comments about being Valentino's crumbs.

But just a little while ago she'd felt the terrible guilt he carried over *his* mother's death. It went so deep she couldn't ignore his plea.

"While your father's alive, you need to make peace with him, Tino. Otherwise you'll always be unhappy."

"I know," came the surprising admission. "Because of you, I've already begun."

Eventually she lifted her head. Pulling out of his arms, she moved herself next to the door. There was something else he had to understand before things went any further. "You do realize that if we were to get married, you could be a widower within the next six months."

The blood left his face. "That's how long Dr. Arno has given you if you don't get a new kidney?"

"Yes."

His features hardened. "I need you in my life, Clara, so that means we're going to have to find you a new one fast!" Valentino's declaration exploded with a ferocity she didn't know he was capable of. He was a fighter; she'd give him that. To have him on her side was like being handed a precious gift. She felt the blood pounding in her ears.

The next thing she knew he started up the truck and they headed for the road leading out of town. He didn't speak again. They eventually turned into the farm and he pulled up to the house.

"Forgive me for keeping you from your bed. I know you're exhausted." He got out of the truck and went around to help her down. "I'll call you tomorrow."

As he started back to the driver's side of the truck she cried, "Don't go yet—"

There was a sharp intake of breath before he wheeled around. She saw a flare of light in the recesses of those dark brown eyes. His reaction astounded her. "I take it that's a yes."

He *knew* it was.

"Shall we go inside together, or do you want to alert your parents first that they're about to have company?"

Her family would be gathered around the table for the evening meal. She couldn't believe this was really happening and moistened her lips nervously. "I'll tell them you're outside waiting to talk to them."

"I swear you won't regret this." Before she could think, he cupped her face between his hands and pressed a warm kiss to her mouth, the first one he'd ever given her. It brought heat to her cheeks she could feel as she broke away from him and hurried inside.

Everyone greeted her as she walked in the kitchen filled with noisy conversation. Her mother eyed her with an anxious expression, probably noticing her heightened color. "You were gone so long, we got worried you missed the bus."

Silvio cast her a questioning glance. Her father patted the empty chair next to him. "Come and eat."

"I've already had dinner, Papa." Her heart thundered in her chest. "Valentino is outside and wants to speak to you and Mamma. Is it all right if he comes in?"

She watched her parents share a surprised look before they nodded.

On less than sturdy legs, she hurried back out to the hall and opened the door. "Tino?"

He came inside and followed her through to the kitchen. After all these years the moment was unreal to see him enter her parents' home at last. Her father stood up. Silvio and Tomaso followed suit.

"Please sit down," Valentino urged them. "Good evening," he said to all of them. "Excuse us for this interruption, but Clara and I decided our news couldn't wait." He moved closer and put his arm around her waist. "Today she agreed to become my wife."

Immediately she heard gasps from everyone, her mother's the loudest.

"There's nothing I want more than to take care of her. With my help, I'm hoping we can find her a matching kidney donor as soon as possible."

She saw her father cross himself.

"You have a right to know my plans. I've given up racing. From now on I'll be helping my father at the restaurant and doing consulting work for my business. For the time being we'll be living at the villa here in Monta Correnti. That way Clara can remain close to all of you."

Silvio paled while her father looked knocked off balance.

"I've already asked Father Orsini to marry us."

At that news Clara almost fainted from shock. He held her tighter.

"Because of her condition, he'll waive the normal waiting period and perform the private ceremony at four o'clock on Saturday at the church. He'll make it short so it won't be hard on her."

She saw her mother start to weep.

"The only people we want in attendance will be your immediate family and mine, provided my father is well enough. If everyone will agree to keep this a secret, there won't be any paparazzi around to ruin it. Do we have your blessing?"

Clara saw her parents stare at each other in amazement before her father turned to them. "Is this what you want, *figlia mia*?"

She took a deep breath. This was truth time. *It's what you* feel *that matters*! her mother had counseled her earlier.

"*Sì.*"

Her father's dark moist eyes swerved to Valentino. "Since my daughter says yes, then I say welcome to the family." He walked around to embrace him and kiss him on both cheeks. Clara's mother joined them.

Valentino kissed her on both cheeks. "Earlier today I told Clara that when I was a boy, I envied her belonging to a happy family like yours. Sometimes she let me eat the delicious food you made for her lunches."

"That's true," Bianca chimed in with a smile on her face. "I watched it disappear, Mamma. Clara made me promise never to tell."

"You're the best cook in Monta Correnti, Signora Rossetti, but I've never told my father that. I let him think the food at Rosa is superior. Secretly I have to tell you I like the idea of belonging to your family."

Clara knew he meant what he was saying. The loss of his mother and the tragic circumstances surrounding her death had blighted his life. She could also see his natural charm was lethal. Already he'd seduced everyone in the kitchen except Silvio, who eyed both of them with a hostile expression.

Valentino turned to her. His gaze played over her with relentless scrutiny. "You look tired. I'm going to leave so you can get to bed. I'll let myself out."

After kissing her cheek, he left the kitchen. She didn't want him to go, but, with the family clamoring to talk to her, it was the only thing to do.

"So," her mother said with a new sparkle in her eyes, "we will have to buy you a wedding dress. I always hoped you would wear mine, but look at you—you're so thin it would fall off you and lie in a puddle on the floor."

Everyone laughed including Clara, who needed to be satisfied with the reason Valentino was marrying her and allow her family to be happy for her. Until a few minutes ago they couldn't have imagined another wedding taking place in the Rossetti family. Neither could she.

"Doesn't it bother you that he didn't propose until you lost all your weight?" Silvio's question stunned everyone.

"No," she answered in complete honesty. "If all he'd wanted was a thin wife, then how come he never married one of the film stars or top models he's been seen with over the years? He's had ample opportunity." He could have married the girl *you* wanted, Silvio—but of course Clara would never have said anything that hurtful to her brother.

His face screwed up in pain. "Just tell me one thing—"

She knew what he was going to ask and took him aside out of earshot. They weren't twins for nothing. Forestalling him, she said, "He needs me, Silvio." Until she'd heard him talking to her mother, she hadn't realized just how much.

Her brother didn't say anything after that, but she knew what was on his mind.

Is he in love with you, Clara? Did he say those words to you? Because if he didn't...

CHAPTER SIX

VALENTINO drove to the restaurant and parked the truck behind the Ferrari. When he stepped inside, he walked over to Giorgio. "The truck's outside filled with gas."

"You didn't have to do that."

"I wanted to. I'm grateful for your help. Do you know where Isabella is?"

"Out in front tabulating the receipts."

"Good. I need to talk to her. See you later. Thanks again for everything." They traded keys.

"*Ciao*, Valentino."

With a nod to the others still cleaning up, he walked through the door into the restaurant.

"There you are," his sister said as soon as she saw him. "Papa is anxious to talk to you."

"Did he find mistakes in the inventory?"

"No. He sounded sorry you ran off so fast."

"That would be a first."

"I told him you had to leave to meet up with Clara."

"Clara's the reason I'm here now. There's something I have to tell you."

"I'm all yours." She finished the last of the receipts and closed up the register. "What's going on?"

He eyed her directly. "Maybe you should sit down. This is important."

A look of alarm crossed over her face and she did his bidding. For the next few minutes he told her about Clara's kidney failure. As he explained the gravity of her condition tears rolled down Isabella's cheeks. "Oh, Valentino. That poor, dear girl."

"I have more news." He sucked in his breath. "Father Orsini is going to marry us in a four o'clock ceremony on Saturday afternoon at the church."

Isabella looked thunderstruck. His stunning revelation actually caused her to drop the money bag she'd been holding. He picked it up for her and put it on the counter.

"I'm not going to let her die if I can help it," he vowed. "Until a kidney is available, she needs help around the clock. The only way to give her the kind of attention she requires is to be with her twenty-four hours a day, so I am going to become her husband."

His sister stared at him in shock. "I don't doubt your sincerity, but what about your racing?"

"Those days are over."

"Just like that?" came her incredulous question.

"I've been considering it for quite a while now."

"Will you live in Monaco?"

"No. At the villa here."

"You're serious—"

"Clara needs her family around. You and Papa need my help at the restaurant."

The blue eyes studying him swam in liquid. "I take back the ugly things I shouted at you the night of Papa's birthday party while you were driving away." So saying, she threw her arms around him and gave him a surprisingly strong hug.

"Don't get ahead of yourself. I'm everything you called me and more, but that girl doesn't have a selfish atom in her entire body. What's happening to her isn't fair."

"It's awful."

"I'm going to find her a kidney if it ends up taking all my money to do it." That was what he intended to tell Dr. Arno when they talked. Clara's doctor still hadn't called him, which meant he hadn't returned from his vacation yet. "Her chances of a long life will be vastly increased if one is found soon."

"Then you *have* to make it happen! You're known for doing the impossible."

"Is that right?"

She smiled. "You know it's true."

"Let's hope this time it is," he ground out. "I'm going to ask the clinician to start training me how to do her dialysis so she can have it at home when we are married. Right now I'm going upstairs to tell Papa I'm getting married."

"He's always wanted you back home. Your news is going to make him happier than you know."

"Happy enough to attend the ceremony with you?" Valentino knew otherwise, but that wasn't important right now. He'd promised Clara he would try to get along with his father. "I'm not sure he's well enough."

"Papa wouldn't miss it. Do you want me to phone Cristiano?"

In the past he'd always let Isabella do everything, but no longer. This was something Valentino had to do himself, though he dreaded it.

"I'll call him," he murmured. "Except for Clara's immediate family, no one else is invited. I don't want Aunt Lisa or our cousins to get wind of it. This has to be kept so quiet the media won't have any idea of it until long after the fact. I'll do anything to prevent the press from intruding on Clara's private agony."

"I understand."

He breathed in deeply. "Once we've said our vows, we'll drive straight to the villa. Fortunately with the church so close, it'll be a quick trip for her."

She put a hand on his arm. "No celebration?"

"Only if Clara is up to it after we're home. I'm leaving that decision to Signora Rossetti."

"You can count on me for any help."

"I know that." His dark brows furrowed. "Too bad you were let down in the younger brother department. From now on I'll try to do better, Izzy."

As he gave her a hug his father entered the empty dining room with his walker.

"What's going on?"

Valentino intercepted Isabella's glance before they moved toward him. "I was just on my way upstairs to talk to you."

"Giorgio told me you were in here. I decided I'd better find you before you ran out again."

"Let's sit down, Papa."

Isabella patted their father's arm. "I'll be right back."

"I don't need to sit. You did an excellent job on the inventory, by the way."

Incredible. "You're the one who taught me."

They eyed each other cautiously. For the first time in his life Valentino got the impression his father seemed nervous of him. He thought back to what Clara had told him about Luca being terrified Valentino would leave town at the first sign of trouble.

His father squinted at him. "You said you had something to tell me?"

"Wouldn't you rather sit? This could take a few minutes."

"All right." He moved the walker to the nearest table and planted himself on a chair. Valentino sat opposite him.

"I've been doing some research to help bring in more business. It's just an idea, but it might be worth investigating."

"I'm listening."

Valentino presented his ideas about the Web site and attracting the tour-bus crowd. When he'd finished his explanation his father pursed his lips. "That's what you and Isabella were hugging about?"

The question wasn't the response Valentino sought. He couldn't tell what his father was thinking, but at least he hadn't rejected the suggestions out of hand. "No. I was saving my other news until last."

"Go on."

"I've been seeing Clara Rossetti since I've been home. She has agreed to be my wife. We're getting married on Saturday at the church and we'll be living here in Monta Correnti. I would like it very much if you could be there." Despite all grievances, he discovered it was true. "However, I know you're not well," he added to give him an out.

His father stared at him for a long time. "She's a fine girl."

"I agree," Valentino said in a husky voice. I'm in love with her. He'd always been in love with her, but he hadn't known until he'd seen her lying there in the clinic and realized she could be taken from him.

"What do you think?" Clara came out of the dressing room wearing a simple white A-line silk gown with a scooped neck and long lace sleeves that covered her graft.

Her mother, bedecked in the pale blue dress she wore to Mass, let out a sound of approval. The tears were never far away. "We bought the right one. You look like a princess."

For once in her life Clara felt like one. It didn't seem possible when just last week she hadn't thought she'd live long enough to see this day. And certainly not with Valentino! How many times in her secret fantasies had she imagined him coming home to Monta Correnti because deep inside he'd always loved her and wanted her for his bride?

When she'd lost all her weight, she'd done it with him in mind. More than anything in the world Clara had wanted to be the beautiful woman on the cover of the magazine standing next to him.

That first day on the stairs when he'd called her Clarissima and told her she was a remarkably beautiful woman, she'd known he'd meant it. She'd seen it in his eyes, in the tone of his voice. It was the look she'd always hoped to see. Today Clara knew a joy so powerful it was already draining her.

Her family had insisted she stay in bed this morning. For once she didn't fight them. They brought her breakfast and lunch. While Bianca did Clara's nails, her mother washed and combed her hair. They wouldn't let her get up until it was time to drive to one of the local bridal shops in Monta Correnti.

Bianca, also in her Sunday best, carried the shoulder-length, matching lace mantilla Clara would put on right before the ceremony. She kissed her cheek. "The gown is perfect on you. I wish all the relatives could come to the church to see you."

"So do I," her mother said with a sigh, "but we'll just have to take pictures for them to see later. Valentino was right about doing everything possible to keep the paparazzi away. So far no one knows anything."

"Except the saleswoman," Clara reminded her.

"Ah—but she has no idea who's going to be your husband."

"And he's going to be upset if we don't get her to the church right now!" Bianca put her arm through Clara's good one. "We need to hurry out to the truck. Papa is waiting."

The three of them made their way to the outside of the shop. Their mother got in the truck first with a bag holding Clara's regular clothes. Bianca helped Clara in next, taking care with her wedding dress, then she got in Tomaso's truck with the children. Silvio had muttered something about meeting them at the church.

Clara's father drove the truck through the town and they followed the winding road up the hillside to the lovely seventeenth-century baroque church of San Giovanni where their family had been attending for generations.

The air was warmer than the day Valentino had driven her to Gaeta. She couldn't have asked for a more beautiful wedding day. While the others were brimming over with excitement—Silvio being the exception—a calm had descended over Clara.

This was a surreal moment for her. Within the hour she would be Signora Casali, a role many women had coveted. She wasn't naïve. Clara understood exactly the unique place she held in Valentino's psyche. She knew what marriage to him meant, and what it didn't mean.

No one wanted to live a long life more than she did. If it wasn't her destiny, then Valentino would be given his freedom soon, but it would be with the knowledge that he'd done everything in his power to keep her alive. She'd witnessed that desire yesterday when Serena had spent the four hours teaching him how to administer Clara's dialysis.

His intelligence allowed him to absorb directions quickly. Valentino was at his best when faced with a challenge. Over the last few days she'd watched him take on this new job of health-care giver with a seriousness and dedication that touched her heart.

That plus his assurance that he was working on his relationship with his father meant more to her than he would ever know. For Luca and him to find peace would guarantee they had a happier marriage. She wanted that with every fiber of her being!

When the end came for her, she had every confidence there'd be no demons to torture him the way they had after his mother had died. In the meantime she planned to devote the time she had left to supporting him around his family and making him as happy as her sickness would allow.

Already she was tired, but that was because this was a day like no other. With so many emotions running rampant inside her, she felt more drained than usual and prayed she'd make it through the ceremony before she wilted.

Her father drove them around the back of the church and pulled to a stop in front of a door used only by the clergy. Tomaso followed in his truck. After the women and children got out, Bianca draped the mantilla over Clara's head. The oohs and ah-h-hs coming from everyone made her smile.

By now her other married brothers, Dante and Cesare, and their families had arrived, bringing her grandmother. She was thankful Tomaso was taking pictures so this day would be preserved.

Father Bruno opened the door and ushered them inside. The younger priest had a serious nature so different from Father Orsini's. Clara got the feeling he didn't approve of this clandestine marriage about to be performed behind doors locked to the public for the next half-hour.

"There you are," Valentino murmured, suddenly appearing in the hallway behind the chapel. He mesmerized everyone as he moved swiftly toward her.

A white rose had been tucked into the lapel of his formal dove-gray suit. Beneath the jacket he wore a darker gray vest. The clothes fit his powerful frame like a glove. In the dazzling white shirt and silk jacquard tie of silver and gray, he could easily have been taken for some important Italian prince. He looked so handsome, her legs almost buckled.

"I can't find the words for how lovely you are," he whispered as his dark, searching eyes played over her face and figure. With that compliment she almost sank to the floor in a puddle, bringing to mind her mother's comment about her wedding dress being too big for Clara.

Valentino seemed to have invisible radar because he put his arm around her waist for support and led her the rest of the way into the chapel. His dark-haired sister Isabella stood nearby.

"Clara? You look beautiful," Isabella said softly and handed her a bouquet of white roses.

"Thank you for coming and for these. The flowers are gorgeous." She buried her face in the petals to hide her emotions while she inhaled their sweet scent.

Next to her sat an imposing Luca Casali with his cane. He'd dressed in a midnight-blue suit for the occasion and looked very distinguished. Valentino helped his father to his feet. The older man patted his son's arm before turning to Clara.

"Welcome to the family," he said in a voice of surprising emotion and gave her a kiss on both cheeks.

"I'm so glad you were well enough to make it," she whispered.

"I wouldn't have missed it and couldn't be more pleased with my son's choice. You were always the best influence on him," he confided sotto voce.

"That's very kind of you to say." He'd sounded as if he meant it. Just then her gaze met Valentino's. Her husband-to-be looked happier than she'd seen him in days. Thank you for coming, Luca. You have no idea what it means to your son and to me.

She wished she could say the same for her twin brother, who sat a few feet away with Maria and the children, unable to pretend something he didn't feel.

While both families greeted each other, Silvio stayed put and only stood up when Father Orsini entered the chapel from a side door. The priest nodded to everyone. "If you will all be seated, I'll ask Valentino and Clara to come and stand in front of me."

Valentino clasped her left hand and drew her toward the priest who'd been their spiritual mentor for the whole of their lives, but the broad smile he'd always had for them was missing. In its place he wore a solemn expression, as if he no longer saw them as children. His wise black eyes seemed to say it was time to put childish things aside for the real test of life.

Father Orsini knew this wasn't a normal marriage between

two young lovers desperate to belong to each other. He was a realist who, though he hoped and prayed for the very best for them, had to consider there would probably be dark days ahead in the near future.

"Clara and Valentino? Normally we would celebrate Mass first, but, considering the unique circumstances, I'm going to marry you now. This will in no way make your marriage less sacred."

She could have kissed the priest for his understanding, but she realized it was Valentino who'd prevailed on Father Orsini to keep the ceremony brief.

The older man cleared his throat. "I have one piece of advice for both of you. Strive to lose yourselves in making the other one happy, then you cannot fail."

Since Clara had already determined to do her part no matter what, it wouldn't be hard to take his advice.

"I see Valentino has already taken you by the hand, Clara. If you'll repeat after me."

Within a few minutes they'd both pledged to love, honor and sacrifice for each other, in sickness and in health. Maybe Valentino didn't realize it—or maybe because he did—his fingers tightened hard around hers when the priest said, 'As long as you both shall live.'

"You wish to exchange rings?"

"*Sì*, Father."

Clara couldn't repress a slight gasp as he produced a gold ring with a brilliant light green stone. He slid it onto the ring finger of her left hand. It fit perfectly.

She in turn waited for Bianca to hand her their grandfather's ring so she could slip it on Valentino's finger. Yesterday morning her grandmother had insisted she take it to give to her intended. It was one of those precious moments in life Clara would always treasure.

Father Orsini nodded. "I now pronounce you, Clara Rossetti, and you, Valentino Casali, husband and wife. In the name of the Father, the Son and the Holy Spirit, Amen."

"Amen." Valentino's deep male voice resonated throughout the chapel. Before she could think, he slid his hands to her shoulders and his mouth descended on hers, sending a river of heat through her already weakened body. It wasn't like the warm kiss he'd given her in front of the farmhouse the other night. With this one she felt unmistakable desire arc through her.

Until now she'd had the impression she was in a strange and beautiful dream, but no longer. All of a sudden this man who'd just become her husband felt so alive and real, she was shaken by powerful new sensations. She broke off their kiss and eased away from him in confusion.

"Are you all right, *piccola?*" She could hear the concern in his voice.

"I'm fine."

"No, you're not. The ceremony has exhausted you. Go with your parents. We'll meet at the villa in a few minutes as planned." They'd agreed it would be better if they weren't seen together leaving the church. Soon enough the world would learn Valentino Casali, the world's most exciting, desirable bachelor, had married a little nobody from a town few had ever heard of.

Clara gave a slight nod. Without looking at him she started for the door where they'd come in a little while ago. She was the first down the passageway and out the back of the church, clutching her bouquet in her hand. Everyone hurried after her and rushed to the trucks parked a few feet away.

Once they were in the cab, her mother cried in alarm, "You look like you're going to faint."

"I'm all right, Mamma."

"We're almost to the villa," her father muttered. "Then you will lie down and have a good rest."

Wrong. Valentino had brought her senses alive. For once in her life, rest wouldn't cure what was wrong with her.

His home was a small, ochre-colored palazzo perched on a summit of vegetation in flower. All the Di Rossi family's royal properties had been built in the prime locations of the region. Any local could point them out, but you couldn't get inside the grounds without passing through the gate.

Valentino had already given her father a remote and directions to the private road leading up to it. Clara's family was still in awe that she would be living in this one with him. For her the only important thing was that she would be an intimate part of his life from now on. The setting was immaterial but lovely as they pulled up to the front with its profusion of flowers and ornamental trees.

Somehow her brand-new husband had beaten them here. He came out the tall paneled doors and pulled her from the truck into his arms.

"Tino—what are you doing?"

He flashed her that devilish smile she remembered from so long ago. "Isn't it obvious?" he murmured against her tender neck.

Once he'd swept her over the threshold, she glanced around her in astonishment. "I've never seen anything so beautiful."

From the elegant foyer to the salon, fresh flowers in every shade possible had been arranged around the period furniture. Flowers reflected in the gilt mirrors, creating the illusion of a wonderful garden.

"You love nature so much, I wanted to bring it inside for our special day."

She was overcome. "I don't know what to say."

"You don't have to say anything. Do you need to go to bed, *piccola*?"

"Not until later." Not after everything you've done to make me happy. "Please put me down."

"Where?"

"How about the love seat over by those tall windows? The view has to be glorious from up here."

Once he'd set her on the small couch and had helped arrange her dress for more pictures, Valentino showed her family through the house. Before long food appeared from the kitchen. He brought her a plate of her mother's cooking. While he sat next to her so they could eat together, Tomaso started taking pictures of the family.

Clara could almost believe she was a normal bride with the normal expectation of a long life with her loving husband and the children who would be born to them.

When she'd eaten all she could, Valentino took her plate. Holding her gaze, he said, "We got away with it, *piccola*. No paparazzi."

"No, thank heaven."

Her father raised his wine glass in salute. "To *all* my married children." He winked at Clara. "I've wanted to say that for many years."

"Papa…" She smiled at him. "Sorry it took so long."

It prompted Valentino to make his own toast. He got to his feet with his powerful legs slightly apart. His gaze fell on Clara. "All good things come to him who waits. To my precious bride."

A blush started at her toes and swept up to warm the crown of her head. With a toast like that coming from such a magnetic personality, there was no question he'd won her family over. But she didn't have to look across the room to feel Silvio's icy glitter.

She'd always been able to read her brother's thoughts…

Valentino's not in love with you, Clara. Personally I can't stand to watch the show he's putting on for the family, let alone that Mamma and Papa are buying into it. Let's not pretend about what's going on here. If you weren't seriously ill, he wouldn't be making a martyr of himself in order to gain the world's attention in a brand-new way.

A new terror seized her heart. Was Silvio right?

Valentino had asked the florist to put flowers in their bedroom. Not as many as in the front of the house, but enough to create atmosphere. While Clara was in the en-suite bathroom taking a shower, he lit the white scented tea-light candles he'd placed around, then he turned out the lights and headed for the guest bathroom at the other end of the hall.

Ten minutes later he returned wearing his navy sweats and discovered her lying under the covers in the middle of the king-sized bed. Her green eyes glowed like jewels above the blue and gold quilt.

"Good evening, Signora Casali."

A smile lit the corners of her mouth. "Good evening, Signor Casali."

"Alone at last."

"My family didn't want to leave."

He sat down on the side of the bed. "It was my idea of the perfect wedding. Short and to the point. The groom gets to whisk away the bride. No endless throngs to navigate. No flash-bulbs going off. Fabulous food, compliments of my new mother-in-law. Of course that's the selfish part of me talking. I'm sorry you couldn't have your best friends and the whole town turn out after the banns were posted."

"I had the part that mattered." She smoothed her hand against the sheet, letting him know she had a lot more on her mind. "Why didn't Isabella and your father come to the house after?"

"Papa told me he felt light-headed after the ceremony. I believed him. He rarely goes anywhere, so Isabella drove him home, but she wanted to come."

Clara eyed him soulfully. "He was very sweet to me."

"How could he not be?"

"I think he was so moved to see you get married, it affected him physically."

"Tonight I'm in the mood to think only the best thoughts, so I'll go along with your take on it."

"Good."

Valentino held up his left hand. "This ring came as a big surprise." He had to wear it on his littlest finger.

"My grandfather had smaller hands than you. Nonna wanted me to give it to you. It's her way of letting you know she approves."

"I'm honored. Now I need to know if *you* do."

"That question was answered the first day we met at school years ago. You made me laugh so hard, the teacher got mad at me instead of you."

"Sorry about that."

"No, you're not," she responded with a quick grin. "You don't need to fish for compliments, but I'll tell one thing if it will make you feel better. You have exquisite taste."

Looking at her right now, he agreed. She was sitting up in bed and rested against the headboard, allowing him a glimpse of the soft pink robe she'd put on. The color added a tint to her creamy complexion, drawing his attention until he couldn't look anywhere else.

"I love my ring." Her hand moved so the facets caught the light from the candles, but he found himself mesmerized by the glints in her dark, silky hair. She'd been blessed with perfectly shaped eyebrows the same color. His gaze fell to the alluring contour of her mouth. The desire to kiss her grew so intense, he was shaken by his feelings and got to his feet.

"I hoped you would like it. Is there anything you want from the kitchen before I put out the candles?"

"Nothing, thank you."

In the next minute he'd blown them out. "Are you tired, *piccola*?" he asked in the darkness.

"I'm happy."

He should have known better than to ask his valiant bride, whose exhaustion had probably reached its peak before their guests left the palazzo. "I want to get to know all your habits so I can be of the most help. When you go to bed at night, what do you normally do?"

"Just what I've done tonight. Take a shower and climb in bed. Usually I'm asleep as soon as my head touches the pillow. What about you?"

"The same, but I usually toss and turn for a while first. When my restlessness is bad, I turn on television. The noise usually puts me out."

"Isn't it strange we've known each other since we were children, yet we don't know all those little things about our everyday lives."

"This is a new adventure for both of us, one I'm already enjoying more than you can imagine. If you'll take the right side of the bed, then I won't worry about rolling onto your arm in the night."

He heard the bedding rustle, then he climbed in and stretched out before pulling the covers over them. Her fragrance was so intoxicating, he feared he'd be walking the floors within the hour.

He turned on his side so he was facing her, but he didn't dare touch her tonight. His fear that she'd push him away was very real. He was still raw from her rejection after he'd taken her to Gaeta. How could he bear it if she accused him of making love to her out of pity? What he needed to do was seduce her slowly; a kiss here, a caress there, until the moment when he knew she wanted all of him.

"Now that I'm your husband, everything has changed. We're going to build a new life together."

He leaned over to kiss her lips. "*Buona notte, mia sposa.*"

CHAPTER SEVEN

WHEN Sunday morning came, Clara was awake before Valentino, whose well-honed body took up most of the bed. In truth, after he'd given her that brief kiss, she'd spent the rest of the night in agony because he hadn't reached for her.

Valentino afraid to make love to her because she was ill? Tears smarted her eyes. She'd give anything to go back to a few days ago when he didn't know about her condition. In the natural progression of things she felt sure he would have started kissing her until neither of them could hold back.

While he slept she was able to study her husband's striking features without his being aware of it. To know she would be waking up next to such an exciting man from now on filled her with intense pleasure, but if he never possessed her, she didn't know how she'd be able to stand it.

Already she loved their new life together so much, the thought of it coming to a quick end because of her illness too unbearable to contemplate. Before she gave in to her emotions and kissed him awake, she slid out of bed and hurried into the bathroom to freshen up and brush her teeth.

With her robe still on, she padded down the hall to the kitchen to fix them a meal. The key was to stay busy. For days now Valentino had been doing everything for her. It was time for him to be the recipient.

Her mother had stocked the fridge with food. All Clara had to do was warm things up and they'd have a feast for breakfast. After making cappuccino, she was ready to go get him when she heard him call out her name.

"I'm in the kitchen!"

He emerged from the hallway in his sweats looking disheveled from sleep and sounding the slightest bit out of breath. The shadow covering his firm jaw made him even more disreputably gorgeous. "Why didn't you wake me?"

"Because you were in a deep sleep and needed it."

She could tell he wasn't in a playful mood. "This wasn't supposed to happen!"

"What? That your wife got up to make breakfast?"

"You know what I mean." That hint of anxiety was in his eyes.

"Tino—when I'm feeling good, I intend to do what comes naturally. If I need help, you'll know about it. Unfortunately you haven't always seen me in top form and it has made you think I'm a twenty-four-hour invalid. Come and sit down."

He was clearly out of sorts and raked a hand through his dark hair before doing her bidding.

"Mamma left us a veritable banquet," she chatted. "I don't know about you, but I'm starving this morning. At our house we always put a little chocolate in the cappuccino. If you don't like it, I'll make you regular coffee."

To her delight he drank a whole mug before lifting his head. At last she saw a smile. "I'll never drink anything else again." On that note he popped two sausage-filled rolls in his mouth. "After we eat, I'm taking us for a scooter ride."

The situation was improving. "On your latest model?"

"I think so."

"I can't wait!"

When he looked at her, she could tell he wanted to ask her if she was sure she was feeling well enough, but he refrained.

She'd never seen his brown eyes so alive. "Neither can I. Even though the temperature's supposed to climb today, we'll dress you warmly."

She finished munching on a roll. "Where are we going to go?"

"Here and there."

Just as they used to do after school. "I'll hurry and get ready."

Valentino devoured two more rolls. "While you do that, I'll shave."

"No, don't—"

His eyebrows lifted.

"I—I mean, you don't have to do it," she stammered.

An unexpected gleam entered his eyes. "You don't mind my scruffy look?"

"It suits you," she mumbled before clearing the table.

"Leave the dishes, Clara. While we're gone the housekeeper will be in to clean up and unpack the bags your parents brought over in the truck. All you need to do is get ready."

By tacit agreement they left the kitchen and walked back to the bedroom. Valentino disappeared in the walk-in closet and brought out some packages he put on the bed. A ghost of a smile hovered around his mouth. "After you're dressed, put all this gear on. We'll see if I bought the right sizes for you."

The second he walked out the door, she pulled underwear, jeans and a cotton sweater from one of her suitcases and was dressed in a flash. In the first bag she found socks and black boots. The next bag contained a woman's stylish leather jacket in white with green side stripes and a mandarin collar. Another bag held matching gloves. In the last large sack she found a woman's helmet.

"Everything fits!" she cried when he came walking in their bedroom a few minutes later carrying his black helmet. He wore black boots and a black leather jacket with blue side stripes. His powerful body looked even bigger in his riding gear. She felt his dark eyes roam over her in male appreciation.

"You have a stunning figure, *piccola*. In an outfit like this, it's dynamite. You'll have to hold me tight around the waist so some dude doesn't pluck you off the back while we're tearing around."

"Tino—" His absurd remark made her laugh.

"You think I'm kidding—" The sudden seriousness of his tone caused her pulse to race. "Have you looked in a mirror lately? Maybe taking you out in public is going to be too dangerous."

"That's what I've thought about you for years." She spoke her mind before she realized what she'd said. In a quick move she dropped the helmet's shield so he couldn't see how red she'd turned. "Shall we go?"

He led her down the hall to the back of the villa. They stepped outside into a small courtyard where she could see the garage. With the remote on his key chain he opened the door. Next to the Ferrari sat a gleaming cobalt blue and gold motor scooter.

Valentino put on his helmet before walking it out into the courtyard. "They brought over the deluxe Tourister. See this pillioned seat?" She nodded. "It lets you ride higher behind me. When I designed this, I had you in mind because you always used to tell me you wished you could see better when we rode around together."

He shouldn't have told her that. It meant too much to her. "The Violetta Rapidita is a beautiful machine, Tino." Her voice caught.

"Wait until you ride on it. You'll be totally comfortable. Climb on behind me."

His excitement infected her. After she got settled and wrapped her arms around his torso she said, "Your mother would have been thrilled to know you named it after her."

When her words computed, he squeezed her mid-thigh. She felt the sensation like a dart of flame. "Outside of my family, no one knows its origin. Nothing escapes you, does it? Are you ready?"

"Yes."

He lifted his hands to put on his leather gloves, then they were off. She felt his imprint long after they'd passed through the gate and were zigzagging down the hillside past the patchwork of charming villas partially hidden by lush foliage.

With one of the world's greatest drivers at the controls, Clara gave no thought to anything but the joy of being alive to share this incredible day with Valentino. Sitting on the scooter put you right next to the earth where you could feel and smell nature, hear all the sounds, yet the higher seat allowed her the full sight of her surroundings.

This was so different than riding in a car or a truck or bus. It took her back to her early teens when he offered her rides home after school or church. Sometimes he'd drive haphazardly on purpose, sending her into peals of laughter while the locals shook their fingers at him. Of course they were much younger then and didn't wear the safety equipment they wore now.

In those days the two of them felt invincible. Was he remembering those matchless moments, too? Half the time his old scooter had let him down and he'd had to walk it or push it. Though she would offer to take a turn so he wouldn't have to do all the work, Valentino always refused. Even then there'd been a chivalrous streak in his nature.

Sometimes they ended up walking all the way to the road leading into the farm. When he waved goodbye and kept walking, she always felt a wrench. In truth she'd been so crazy about Valentino, if he'd asked her to go on a walk around the world with him, she would have gone.

Clara had dreamed her dreams, but she could never have imagined that over a decade later she would end up being his wife, riding pillion on this streamlined version of comfort and perfection he'd invented. She nestled tighter against him, resting her chin on his shoulder to feel his body and prove to herself he was flesh and blood, not a fantasy conjured in her imagination.

"Are you all right?" he called to her, turning his head to the side.

"I'm wonderful!" she shouted back. "This is heaven!"

At her comment he twisted the throttle, accelerating them around the next curve where the countryside opened to their gaze. Euphoric, they whizzed past manicured fields and vineyards. Without a cough their scooter ate up the kilometers of rolling hills.

Before long they veered onto a farming road rarely used by tourists. It eventually circled around the furthest end of her family's lemon groves. There was no sight like the straight rows of twenty-foot trees thriving in the sun. Delectable yellow fruit peeked out from the dark green foliage.

It was at the top of one of the trees she could see in the distance where she'd cut her leg, but she didn't want to think about that right now. Please no shadows. Not today.

Valentino didn't slow down. He kept heading south past other farms and cypress trees. This whole area burgeoned with nature and represented paradise to her. She couldn't get enough of it. Eventually they came to the shimmering blue water of Lake Clarissa. Valentino had grown up along this shoreline.

She'd driven past his home many times out driving in her family's truck with Bianca, but that had been when Valentino was winning races in other parts of Europe or the States. Clara had yet to see the inside of his home; knowing it held one of the most painful memories for him, she could understand why he didn't want to stay there now.

He drove them around the west end. When they came to a lay-by, he pulled into it and shut off the motor. They both removed their helmets to take in the lake's beauty. There was a path leading through a meadow-like patch to the water.

Anxious to follow it down, she swung her leg over and climbed off the scooter.

"I think we'll rest here and enjoy a snack." He fastened their helmets to the bars, then opened the trunk. To her surprise he'd packed a light blanket. Beneath it she discovered bottled water, apples and a carton of chocolate biscotti. He must have made preparations after she'd fallen asleep last night.

"You remembered—" she cried in awe before reaching for it. "I haven't eaten these since the last time you got sick after splurging on three packs at once."

He tossed back his dark head and laughed. It was a man's deep belly kind of laughter. She felt it rumble through her nervous system with a sense of wonder.

"If you noticed, I only bought one this time. I can't risk becoming indisposed when I'm driving such precious cargo around."

"Indisposed hardly describes your former condition," she quipped to cover her emotions, which were jumping all over the place. Gathering the other items, she started toward the path.

A chuckling Valentino followed her. Several feet from the shore of the lake he spread the blanket over the wild grass and they both sank down. She whipped off her gloves so she could open her water and drink. "Um. That tastes good."

"It does," he agreed after swallowing half of his in one go.

Clara fell back against the blanket and stared up at the sky, where she could see clouds building. "There's going to be a storm later today."

He lay down next to her and opened the carton. "Then it's good we came out here early."

Suddenly he rolled on his side, bringing him breathtakingly close. Without saying anything, he put a cookie to her lips. There was a mirthful glimmer in his eyes. She took a bite. He finished it off and fed her another one.

After three bites she couldn't keep up with him. "No more."

"No? Then how about a different treat?"

"I think I'll save the apple for later."

"I wasn't thinking of fruit." The amusement she'd seen had faded. In its place she glimpsed something else that made her mouth go dry and sent pleasure pains to her palms. "In the past you and I did just about everything together, but we never played six minutes in *paradiso* or spin the *bottiglia da vino*."

A smile turned up the corners of her mouth. "That's because you were too busy playing those games with every other girl in our class. It made the boys furious. As I recall Aminta, Bettina and Crocetta were all enamored of you at the same time."

He traced the line of her mouth with his finger. "I've grown up since then and have developed an appetite for a new treat. Be kind to me, *piccola*."

Valentino didn't give her time to think before he covered her mouth with his own. For once she didn't want to think. His playful mood had infected her, making her want to give in to the sensuous side of her nature. She had one, but had never allowed herself permission to enjoy what other girls took for granted.

Now that there was a time bomb ticking away inside her, she didn't want to leave this world never having known this pleasure with Valentino. "If it's kindness to kiss you back, then I can't think of anything I'd like to do more."

His jacket was open. She slid her hands up his chest and wrapped them around his neck to get closer. In a slow, sweet rhythm she began responding to the urgency of his demands. The pressure of his mouth invading hers melted her insides, sending a languorous warmth through her body.

This was what she'd been waiting for last night. It was ecstasy. She knew what the word meant and had an intellectual knowledge of it, but now that she was experiencing it she didn't want to do anything else. The freedom to do whatever she desired had taken hold of her.

He was such a beautiful man she needed to kiss every centimeter of his face. The best way to do that was to slide on top of him in order to find those favorite spots. She wished they weren't wearing their leather jackets, but she was too enraptured to take the time to remove hers.

"When did you get this scar?" she asked some time later, having discovered it while she was kissing his eyelids.

"I don't remember," he answered in a husky voice. "At sea, I think."

He reversed their position so he was half lying on top of her. "There's not a mark on your skin anywhere. It's like a baby's. Absolutely like velvet and flawless. Everything about you is flawless."

Clara raised her head to kiss the end of his nose. Unused to his compliments, she said, "Except on the inside." But the second the words were out, she regretted them.

With that slip, the enchantment of the moment was gone—not for her, but for him. She knew it by the way he checked himself before moving away from her and lying back on the blanket.

She couldn't bear for this to end and leaned over him. "Don't you want to play anymore?"

Valentino *had* been playing with his wife. He'd never enjoyed anything so much in his life. But if this was just a game to her to make *him* happy, then it changed the rules.

He hated games.

Clara wasn't like other girls who'd passed through his life. She'd been the different one. *His rock.* You didn't trifle with her kind.

When he dug deep down, he realized he didn't want her trifling with him. Anyone else, but not his *piccola*.

Not unless she meant it.

With this new weight troubling him, he felt confused and restless. He raised his hand to smooth some of the hair away from her flushed cheek. "I could play with you all day, but the sky's getting darker and the temperature has dropped. We can't afford to get caught in a storm. The last thing you need is to come down with a cold."

Valentino saw the glint of pain in her eyes before she moved away and got to her feet. Her kidney disease was a fact of life. Since leaving the villa he'd been the one to live in denial. Yet not even the game he'd started—the game he knew she'd enjoyed and would still enjoy if they continued— could make either of them forget. That would be asking the impossible.

Ten minutes after they'd arrived back at the villa, the rain started. While Clara disappeared into the shower to get warmed up, Valentino heated the chicken and pasta her mother had brought.

As soon as lunch was over they were expecting an important visitor. His wife would be surprised, but he knew it would be a good one. "Clara? Lunch is ready," he called to her.

"I'm coming." Within seconds she appeared in the kitchen dressed in a thin light blue cotton wrapper like the one she'd worn last night. It had long sleeves and fell to her knees, barely hinting at the lovely mold of her body beneath. Evidently it was a style and weight she found comfortable for her treatments. "This looks delicious, Tino. Thank you."

"We have your mother to thank for a few more days, then the real test will come when you have to survive on my cooking."

One graceful eyebrow lifted. "You mean *our* cooking. We'll be sharing the work around here."

He let her comment pass and poured them coffee before sitting down at the table with her. Their morning jaunt had depleted her strength. She would never admit it unless she had to, but he'd been around her long enough to tell when she was getting tired. Her eyelids fluttered a little and she lost some color.

As they were finishing the last of their food, he heard the sound of a vehicle pulling up in the rear courtyard. Clara heard it, too, and looked at him in surprise since no one could enter the grounds without authorization. "Are you expecting someone?"

He nodded. "I set the master switch to open the gate. Sit still and I'll get the door."

Once outside, he greeted Serena and the two other clinicians who'd come with her. After telling her she'd find Clara in the kitchen, he helped the men unload the mobile dialysis machine and wheel it into the villa.

They were good people to come on a Sunday. Even though he was paying them a great deal extra for this service, he was grateful Clara would be able to get a treatment today and wanted them to know it.

He could hear the two women talking and took advantage of the time to show the men to the bedroom where they could set up the machine. Valentino's work with Serena had been instructive.

If Clara could do a longer, slower dialysis every night while she slept, not only would it free up her days and give her more energy, it wouldn't be as hard on her body. She wouldn't get as many cramps and she'd suffer less nausea. Except for a new kidney, he couldn't ask for more than that during this interim.

Serena was scheduled to work with Valentino this afternoon, then the men would each come for two nights to continue training him. By then he'd be able to take care of Clara himself. Provided God was in his heaven, she wouldn't need dialysis once a kidney had been found.

"Hi," his wife said softly as she came in the bedroom with Serena, her gaze finding Valentino's. "This was an amazing surprise considering it's a Sunday. Thank you. All of you," she added the last. Her moist green eyes reflected her gratitude. It brought a boulder to his throat.

"Shall we get started?" Serena asked. "Since you'll be getting a longer treatment tonight, we'll do a shorter session now. Clara? While you get comfortable on the bed and roll up your sleeve, I'll ask Valentino to wash his hands, then put on rubber gloves. We'll leave a box of them in the bathroom."

Three hours later everyone left with the proviso that Carlo would be back at eleven p.m.

Valentino saw them out, then went back to the bedroom with some juice and a roll for Clara. She was sitting up against the pillows. Her color was somewhat improved. He put her food on the bedside table next to her. "How do you feel?"

"I was just going to ask *you* the same question."

"If you want to know the truth, I'm relieved we've gotten this far."

"You've taken on a huge responsibility." Her voice throbbed.

"It's what I wanted."

She eyed him soulfully. "I believe you, but that doesn't make it any easier on you."

"The job itself isn't difficult."

Her brows formed a delicate frown. "Tell me what's troubling you the most."

"It's something Serena said."

"What was that?"

"She said that humans might have invented a dialysis machine to filter out the impurities that our kidneys can't, yet it can only do fifteen percent of the job done by a four-ounce kidney God created. We're going to find you a kidney, Clara," he whispered almost savagely. "I won't rest until then."

She patted the bed. "I'm the luckiest woman in the world to be married to you. Come and lie down by me. You look tired. Don't deny it."

He flashed her a wry grin. "I won't."

While she ate and drank, he stretched out next to her and closed his eyes. A few minutes later he felt her fingers furrow through his hair. Her touch electrified him. "Did I tell you I had the most wonderful day of my life today?"

Valentino grasped her hand. "Would you believe me if I told you I felt the same way?"

"They say you can't go back, but we did."

His lids opened. "Now I'm anxious to move forward with you. While we were riding on the back roads, I saw that the old Brunello place was for sale."

"I noticed it, too. It used to be a beautiful little farmhouse, but now it's run down. The small lemon grove has been sadly neglected." After she eased her hand from his, she looped her arms around her raised knees covered by the quilt. "Can you imagine any family being willing to give up their land?"

"Maybe there was no one to inherit."

She made a funny sound in her throat. "In the Rossetti family, that would be unheard of."

"In the Casali family, too, believe me." They both smiled. "If you're feeling good tomorrow, how would you like to drive back there and walk around to get a feel for it?"

A curious look crept into her eyes. "Are you thinking of buying it for an investment?"

"I'd like to buy it for us so we can live there."

Clara looked shaken. "I don't understand. What about this villa?"

"It belongs to the Di Rossi family. When Isabella begged me to come home, she talked to her fiancé, Max, about letting me rent it. I was saved the trouble of having to find a furnished place."

"I didn't realize you hadn't bought it."

"There are many things we still don't know about each other. Little did I expect that as soon as I got here, I'd become a married man so fast. Now I want a home of my own to put down roots and build a life with you."

She scrambled out of bed. "But you own a fabulous villa in Monaco. I've seen pictures of it in *Hello* magazine."

"When I made enough money from the motor-scooter sales, I bought it for an investment, but I rarely live there. Maybe this weekend we can drive there and stay over one night before I sell it. Though the economy is poor, I'm still pestered by a few interested parties who are anxious to take it off my hands. I'll put the money to good use on our own plot of ground."

"But, Tino," she cried, "you're not a farmer!"

"Maybe not, but I'm married to a farmer's daughter and Monta Correnti is home to me, too. Does the idea have any appeal, *piccola*?"

Clara's eyes slid away from his. When shadows darkened her features, he felt as if a giant hand had just cut off his oxygen supply. "Of course it does," came a small voice, "but I'm afraid you're getting ahead of yourself."

Her comment coincided with the ringing of his cell phone. Her crushing reply, guaranteed to stifle all hope of a long life together, turned his mood dark. He finally got off the bed and pulled it out of his pocket.

"It's your family," he said after glancing at the caller ID. "Your phone must be turned off. While you talk to them, I'll make certain the house is closed up for the night." He tossed the phone on the bed before striding out of the bedroom.

She sank down on the side and reached for it. "Hello?"

"Clara? Are you all right? Valentino told us he'd arranged for you to start your dialysis at home today."

"He did, Mamma. Serena just left. I—I couldn't be better." Physically it was true. Getting another treatment this afternoon instead of having to wait until tomorrow had already made a difference in how she felt.

Because of Valentino she wouldn't have to go to the clinic anymore. From now on she'd sleep through her treatments and start to live life during the day like a normal person. But the situation with him was unraveling fast. Twice today she'd said something to ruin the moment. Father Orsini had counseled her to make her husband happy.

"You're doing a great job, Clara."

"What did you say?" her mother asked.

"Sorry. I was thinking out loud. Thank you for all the wonderful food. Valentino sings your praises."

"He's a wonderful man." *I know.* "Even your father says so."

Her parents would be overjoyed if they knew about his plans to purchase some farming property. She was in awe of his unselfishness, not just because money wasn't his raison d'être, but because he gave of himself.

Tonight he would have to stay up and work with Carlo till four in the morning while he was trained to perform this service for her. Tears sprang to her eyes and wouldn't stop running down her cheeks.

"Clara? Are you crying?"

"Yes."

"Because he makes you so happy, *sì*? He does everything for you."

"Yes." Her husband did his duty better than any husband alive. It was time she did something for him in return.

"Both Gina and Lia phoned. I hope it's all right that I told them you got married."

"Of course. I'll call them tomorrow."

"By now your father has told everyone else in the family."

Clara smiled. "Pretty soon the word will get out and it will be all over the news. Don't be surprised if the paparazzi come by the farm for an interview and pictures."

Her mother laughed. "Come visit us soon."

"We will, Mamma, and we'll have you come to the villa for dinner. Tell Papa and Bianca I love them, and tell Nonna that Valentino loves his ring."

"That will make her happy."

She bit her lip. "How's Silvio?"

"Grumpy. He misses you."

"I lived in Naples for a long time. He didn't miss me then."

"Oh, yes, he did, but this is different, and *you know why*," she whispered.

Just then her brother's nemesis walked in the bedroom. She needed to talk to him. "Kiss little Paolito for me. *Buona notte*, Mamma."

Wiping the moisture off her face, she hung up. "My parents send their love."

A mask had descended over his arresting features. He took the phone from her. "No doubt they're worried about you."

"Actually they think I'm in the best of hands, which I am." Her voice trembled. "Talking with Mamma brought your father to mind. Could we go visit him tomorrow after we've been out to the Brunello farm?"

He placed his phone and wallet on top of the dresser. "I think we'd better put both those ideas on hold for the time being."

"I don't want to," she said with a pounding heart. He darted her a quizzical glance. "You'll have to forgive me for speaking so impulsively earlier. Ever since I was diagnosed, I'm afraid I stopped planning for a future and have been trying to be content by living day-to-day."

His mouth thinned. "In your shoes I would probably do the same thing."

"But we're husband and wife now, and I'm not the only person in this marriage. Naturally you're not going to be content renting a place when you could have your own home in the countryside we both love. It was shortsighted of me. Please let's drive out there tomorrow and look at the house."

To her relief Valentino rubbed the back of his neck, a sign that he was thinking, listening. "I'll phone the realtor in the morning and we'll go from there."

"Good!" She was pleased he'd agreed to that much. "Do you think your father's too sick for company?"

"No."

When he didn't say anything else she said, "You're tired. I'm going to go in the study and watch television while you get some sleep. The bed in this room is bigger than the one in the guest bedroom. Eleven o'clock will be here before you know it."

She started to leave, but he called her back. "Now I'm the one who's sorry. Forgive me for being abrupt with you." His eyes narrowed on her face. "We'll go over to the restaurant tomorrow only if you're up to it."

"You don't have to apologize for anything."

"Of course I do. You made a perfectly normal suggestion to drop in on my father, but there are things you still don't know."

There was more?

"It meant a lot to me that he came to our wedding, but I still struggle. Bear with me."

"You know I will. Tell me the rest."

He nodded. "Papa and Lisa have never gotten along. Being business rivals, you don't know what it's like when they're together. They have this way of going for the jugular."

"That's horrible."

"Before long their squabbling grows into a major conflict

that makes everyone so uncomfortable you want to run for your life. I ran to you a lot during those times. Isabella reminded me I preferred your company to anyone else's."

The revelation took Clara by surprise. She didn't know what to say.

"Growing up I had the sense that something ugly had occurred for them to be at each other's throats all the time. Sure enough it all exploded the night of my father's birthday party. Isabella and I heard angry voices coming from the courtyard. You'd think the party would have given them a reason to try to get along for one night."

He sprang from the bed, unable to sit still. "We got up to investigate. I could hear my aunt announcing to anyone listening that not all my father's children had shown up for the party. She was baiting him relentlessly.

"Isabella and I thought she meant Cristiano, but then she said, 'It's time the secret was out, Luca!' Papa tried to shush her up, but she just kept talking. 'Your children don't know you have two older sons! Don't you think it's time they found out?'"

"What?" Now Clara was on her feet and moved closer to him.

His body tensed. "It seems my father had twins with his first wife, Cindy. She was an American and after their divorce went back to live in the States. Father kept the twins with him for a while, but then, for some reason, he sent them to live with their mother in America and he never bothered to tell any of us about the boys. Of course Aunt Lisa knew all about it and took great delight in exposing his secret. She'd seen the one named Angelo in the newspaper back in New York. The other one is called Alessandro."

Twins. "How old are they?"

"Thirty-eight. Papa gave them up at the time of the divorce. When he married my mother and the three of us came along, he never breathed a word about them."

"No one else ever mentioned them?"

He shook his head. "I found out our cousin Lizzie knew, but she was little at the time and Aunt Lisa told her to keep quiet about it. My aunt has a cruel side. So does my father apparently. I'm not saying he wasn't good to me, but I'm having a hard time dealing with the fact that he has two other children he's never acknowledged."

Luca Casali was an enigma to Clara. There had to be an explanation for a man who could accept Violetta's love child as his own and raise him, yet abandon his oldest flesh and blood sons and pretend they didn't exist.

Clara was desperate to ease her husband's pain. Knowing he wasn't Luca's blood son had made Valentino insecure his whole life. Now to learn about two older brothers had raised all those old issues of jealousy and feeling inadequate.

Maybe one day when emotions weren't running as high, she'd be able to talk to him about it, but right now Valentino was in no state to hear anything. All she could do was listen.

"Would you believe my sister wants to get to know them?"

Yes. As long as Clara had known her, Isabella had been a do-gooder. She'd been raised as Luca's biological daughter, so she didn't have the same emotional struggles as Valentino. But again Clara had to keep those thoughts to herself.

She put a hand on his arm. "Under the circumstances, do you have any idea how much I admire you for coming back home to help your family? For trying to make peace with your father? You had every right to stay away and refuse to deal with the problems. You could have excluded your father from our wedding. But you didn't do any of those things. That's because you're a real man, Tino."

Rising on tiptoe, she kissed his hard jaw and headed for the study.

CHAPTER EIGHT

WHILE Clara was fixing their breakfast the next morning, the long-awaited call from Dr. Arno came through. Valentino took it in the bedroom where he could talk to him in private.

"Thank you for phoning me, Doctor."

"You're very welcome. I'm sorry you had to wait so long. It isn't often I get someone as famous as Valentino Casali asking me to call him back. I'm a keen fan of yours."

"Thank you very much."

"My receptionist told me you're an old friend of one of my patients."

"Yes. In fact Clara and I were just married."

"*Married*?"

"Yes. We did it quickly so I could be with her around the clock to help her."

"Well, congratulations. She's a courageous young woman. A lovely one, too. You're a lucky man."

"I couldn't agree more. If you have time now, I'd like to hear anything you have to tell me about her condition that Serena might not have shared. Most of all I want to know how I can help find Clara a donor sooner."

"I understand your impatience, Signor Casali, but be assured our department is doing everything humanly possible for her.

Since her family hasn't been able to produce one, I'm hopeful we'll find her an altruistic donor."

A tight band constricted Valentino's breathing. "I've thought everything over and would like to be one *if* it's possible."

"She has Type O blood. What's yours?"

Valentino's heart did a kick. "The same. I'm in perfect health. No weight problem, no high blood pressure, no history of diseases, no steroid use, no tobacco, no drugs, recreational or otherwise. Dr. Rimbaud in Monaco will send you all my medical records."

"You sound too good to be true."

"Except that I'm not related to her."

"That isn't necessarily a problem. Over the last several years, immunosuppressive medications have improved to the extent that our transplant center often considers poor tissue matches between donors and recipients. Certainly a kidney matched at four, five or six antigens from a family member may do better in the long term than others, but, as I said, the new medications are proving highly effective."

He gripped his phone tighter. "In that case, let's move ahead immediately."

"Can you come to the hospital in Rome for tests tomorrow?"

"I'll be there in the morning." He would tell Clara he had business. Maybe she could spend the time with her family.

"That's wonderful. I'll set everything up for you and we'll get started on your blood work."

"How long before the transplant can actually take place?"

"If all looks good, I'd say seven to ten days."

"How involved is the surgery?"

"Obviously not as much for you as for Clara, but there are always those normal risks. We have a new technique that takes around three hours and is not as invasive. You'll both be in the hospital four to five days to recover.

"During the transplant operation, you'll both be under a general anesthesia and administered antibiotics to prevent possible infection. Once the new kidney is attached, I may or may not remove her diseased ones. It all depends on the circumstances surrounding her kidney failure. Barring complications, you'll both leave the hospital to face a normal life."

A normal life.

Relief swamped him that they might be able to have a normal life and everything that went with it. "I don't want Clara to know anything about this yet. We can tell her when the time comes, not before."

"That's a very wise decision for both your sakes. If it turns out you're not a good candidate for some reason we don't know about yet, then there's no point in getting either of your hopes up. Before she knows anything, I'd like us to be absolutely certain of optimum results. But I can tell you this much—your being a live donor will give her twice the chance of recovery since your kidney will be healthy and fresh."

Just hearing that made him want to get the surgery done as soon as possible. He thanked the doctor, eager to follow through with his plans.

Clara waved to the realtor as she and Valentino left the Brunello farm on the scooter under more overcast skies. "The man is besotted by you, *piccola*. In that cherry-red cotton sweater you're wearing, I can't say I blame him."

"Don't be silly." She wished her body didn't react every time he made a personal remark. Clara thought it was only redheads whose emotions were too close to the surface. "He's old enough to be my grandfather."

"Didn't you know they have the worst fantasies?"

She chuckled, aware she was feeling different this morning. Better. For the first time in weeks she'd awakened without a hint of nausea. Two treatments since yesterday when she normally wouldn't have had one until today proved the effectiveness of nighttime dialysis. Only Valentino could have made this possible.

He had to be exhausted after his five-hour vigil last night, but he hadn't shown it while they'd inspected the farmhouse. What a disappointment it had turned out to be. The whole place reeked of neglect and was in much worse shape than she'd thought. They'd left without giving the realtor any indication of their true feelings. Naturally Valentino wanted to keep looking.

While she was deep in thought, he said, "On our way back to town, I'd like to stop at your parents' long enough to get that sample of limoncello you told me about. We're almost there now."

"How did you even remember?" Clara had thought he was going to suggest they find a newspaper and see what else was for sale in the Monta Correnti area.

"I've been salivating for a taste of it ever since you mentioned it."

A dissenting sound escaped her lips. "You made that up to make me feel good."

"I'm glad if it did, but, to tell you the truth, the few times I've been served it, I haven't been impressed."

"Now I'm afraid."

"Not you—you're the most courageous person I've ever known. You *are*, you know, so humor me," he said in his deep voice. "It's possible the daughter of Signora Rossetti, who cooks the best food I've ever tasted, has inherited her mamma's special gift."

"You're so full of it, it's no wonder my mother is crazy about you. She'll be thrilled to see us."

A few minutes later they pulled up to the farmhouse. Valentino waited for her to alight. After they took off their helmets, they went inside. Maria was in the kitchen feeding lunch to her youngest and to Paolito, who was in the high chair.

Clara gave them kisses, then hugged her sister-in-law. "Where's Mamma?"

"Giving Nonna a bath because Bianca is too sick."

"Is it her nausea?"

"That and her pain. Tomaso took her to the clinic. It sounds like a bladder infection."

"I know about those." Clara's voice shook.

Valentino slid his arm around her shoulders and pulled her close. "I'm sure she'll be all right, *piccola*."

"Of course she will," Maria assured her.

"If you and Mamma need help, Valentino and I can stay."

"No, no. Everything's fine."

"If you're sure."

Maria smiled. "You two are still on your honeymoon." But it wasn't the kind Clara's sister-in-law was talking about. "I'll tell Mamma and Bianca you came by."

She nodded, still uncertain.

"Where's the limoncello? I'll get it," Valentino whispered.

"Oh—I forgot. It's right over here." She moved out of his hold and found the corked bottle in the cupboard by the door. She found a sack to put it in. After handing it to him she hurried over to give the children another kiss. "I'll call Bianca later to see how she is."

"She'll probably be home in another hour."

"*Ciao*, Maria," Valentino called out from the doorway.

"*Ciao*, Valentino."

Clara followed her husband out to the scooter. He gave her a kiss on the neck while she was putting her helmet back on. "Do you want me to drive to the clinic in case she's still there?"

"No, Tino, but thank you for offering. She'd think I was crazy. It's just that they've all been wonderful to me, especially Bianca."

They headed down the drive for the main road. "You two were always close. I'm afraid I can't relate where Cristiano is concerned."

"I'm so sorry." She'd give anything to help him.

"Don't be. I shouldn't have brought him up."

"I'm glad you did," Clara said, emotion clear in her voice. "You need to talk about it."

"Now you're spoiling *me*," he bantered.

"It's about time. What you need is a long nap after being up all night."

"Only if we do it together."

Clara couldn't wait until lunch was over. Sleeping or waking, she craved every second being with her husband.

The next afternoon, Valentino returned from his visit with Dr. Arno in Rome and walked in the kitchen to find Clara just getting off the phone with her friend Gina. He wore an expectant look on his handsome face. "How good do you feel?"

It wasn't an idle question. "Happy now that you're back from Rome. Did your business go well?"

"Better than expected. I think Papa is going to be surprised when I tell him several more tour operators are considering his restaurant very seriously."

"That's wonderful!"

He smiled. "Feel like getting out?"

"I've got lots of energy if that's what you're asking."

"Then I'm going to let you do the honors." He put the Ferrari keys in her hand.

She blinked. "I wouldn't dare drive your car."

"*Our* car," he corrected her. With his hands spanning her waist, he held her a few inches above the ground. "Say it."

"Tino—put me down."

"Say it!"

"All right. *Our* car."

"That wasn't so hard, was it?" He pressed a surprisingly hungry kiss to her mouth before walking her outside to the driver's side of the Ferrari. After he opened the door for her, she was so dizzy with reaction she almost fell into the black leather seat.

He joined her in a minute. She stared helplessly at him.

"Get into the harness first."

After she managed to do that, he fastened the lap belt, then kissed her lips again. He was no stranger to intimacy, but this was new to Clara. He needed to stop doing that or she wouldn't be able to concentrate.

"Tino—I don't know what to do—"

"Sure you do. You've driven a truck before. You can drive this. Feel down the side of the seat and press the button forward until you're close enough."

Going on faith, she reached down. To her surprise it worked just the way he'd said.

"Bravo. Now put the key in the ignition and turn on the power." As soon as she did it, the car came alive like a beautifully tuned instrument. "It's automatic. Just put it in drive. No clutch to worry about."

Pressing her lips together, she did his bidding. The car crept forward. She turned right at the end of the alley and joined in the mainstream traffic. At first she was terrified, but after a few minutes of navigating through the center of town she started to feel braver.

"You're doing fine, *piccola*. There's the sign for Lake Adrina. Let's head that way. If you get too tired, I'll take over."

Tired? What was that? This was so thrilling, she felt that any second now they were going to take flight.

Little by little they left the traffic behind until she couldn't see any cars, then she pressed on the accelerator. The car took off like a rocket, causing her to cry out in sheer delight. Valentino's face had broken into a broad smile. For the moment he looked so carefree, it filled her with joy.

"Oh—I can't believe it! This is the most fun I've ever had in my life!" The car hugged the curves. Her confidence grew as she passed slower cars and trucks. Clara could see the needle on the speedometer climbing, but she didn't care. In no time at all the lake appeared in the distance. They'd already come fifty kilometers!

Valentino leaned closer to her. "Do you want to stop for a drink?"

"No!"

More laughter poured out of him.

She could have gone around the lake, but the drive back to town would allow her to go a lot faster, so she turned and headed back toward Monta Correnti. "I never understood your love of speed, but I do now!" Already she was addicted.

Halfway back she heard sirens, but didn't associate them with her driving until two police cars pulled alongside her. "Uh oh. Tino—" The officer in front motioned to her that she should pull off the road. "How can I stop when the road is this narrow?"

"Do it anyway," he answered in a calm voice. "It's their problem, not yours. After you've stopped, put the window down and start looking for your driver's license."

Valentino had obviously been through this experience before. Hot and flustered, she pulled to the right as far as she dared, then slowed to a stop. Immediately four officers got out. Two waved the traffic past them, while the other two approached the car.

"Do you have any idea how fast you were going, *signorina*?" the older one with the moustache demanded, but the second he saw Valentino a look of shock altered his fierce expression. He turned to the other officers. Soon everyone knew the famous Valentino Casali was in the car.

"*Mi dispiace tanto*, Signor Casali. We didn't realize it was you."

By this time Valentino had put down his window. "That's all right. My *squisita* bride has been dying to drive my car. Today she took it into her head to take off with it when I wasn't looking. I had to run to catch up with her."

That brought a roar from the men.

"It's a good thing you stopped her when you did because I was starting to get nervous. I was never this nervous at the track."

"Tino!" His comment had the officers reeling with laughter.

They each took turns going around to his side to talk to him about his last race. One of them got a camera from his police car and started taking pictures. She could tell they were ecstatic to have met their favorite hero. Finally the same officer tore himself away long enough to talk to her.

"I'll only give you a warning this time, Signora Casali," he said with a smile.

"Did you hear that, *bellissima*?" He'd undone his harness and leaned over to give her a lingering kiss on the lips. "You're very fortunate they are being so kind to you. Thank them nicely, *per favore*."

While she muttered something indistinct, they took pictures of her, of them, of the Ferrari. If the officers didn't have a job to do, they'd have probably hung around Valentino all afternoon and evening. No doubt they'd never pulled over a celebrity as famous as her husband.

When all the *arrivederci*s had been said and they'd driven off, she finally found herself alone with Valentino. "They did us a great favor today. I saw the way that officer was looking at you. It's a good thing I married such a beauty or your punishment could have been a great deal worse."

Too many emotions were fighting for expression. She

squinted at him and could tell his shoulders were shaking. "I'm glad you think this is so funny."

"Don't you? I knew you were brave, but I never dreamed I had such a little daredevil on my hands."

"Neither did I," she admitted before she found herself laughing, too. "It's the car's fault."

"That's as good an excuse as I've ever heard." Their shared laughter filled the empty spaces in her heart.

She started the car and they took off again, but she forced herself to stay within the speed limit. When they reached the town she had the feeling they were being followed.

"Tino?"

"I've already seen them. It's the paparazzi. They no doubt listened in on the police band. We've been found out. Keep driving to the villa. They won't be able to follow us past the gate."

He was so used to being followed and harassed, she could tell he took it in his stride, but this was a new experience for her. "I wish I were in a tank, then I'd mow them down until they resembled a sheet of aluminum foil."

"Putting you behind the wheel has brought out the spitfire in you. I would never have believed it." Valentino was still chuckling after they'd parked the car and gone inside the house.

Once inside he fastened his dark brown eyes on her. "I'm starving and imagine you are, too."

"I have to admit our adventure has given me an appetite."

"Good," he said, getting down two small liqueur glasses. "This is the perfect time to try out your homemade aperitif. A good appetizer should improve our meal." He pulled the cork from the bottle sitting on the counter and inhaled the aroma. "I can smell your family's lemon grove."

Her pulse sped up. "It's the taste that's important. I hope it won't put you off your food."

He poured a little of the yellow liquid into each glass, then took a drink and savored it for a moment before swallowing all of it. She watched him nervously before he poured himself another glass.

Like déjà vu he lifted it. "I'd like to propose a toast." His penetrating gaze sought hers. The way he was looking at her made it difficult to breathe. "To the success of my brilliant wife."

"At least you didn't choke on it." She clinked her glass with his and they both drank. "You're a terrific sport."

His expression sobered. "I don't think you understand. This liqueur is going to put your name on the map."

She smiled. "I don't want it to be on the map, but you're very sweet to say so."

Lines marred his features. "I'm not sweet at all. You've got a recipe here someone would kill for. Does your teacher at the college have a copy of it?"

His question surprised her. "No."

"Do any of the students?"

"No."

"Where is it?"

"In my school notebook at the farm."

"We'll pick it up tomorrow." He put the cork back in the bottle. "This needs to be kept in a safe place."

While he put it in one of the cupboards, she started getting a meal ready. Soon they were able to sit down and eat. She kept looking at him while he devoured his food.

"You're acting preoccupied just like you used to when you were working on your scooter designs. What's going on?"

"This and that," he murmured evasively.

He wouldn't tell her about his trip to Rome until he was ready. "You sound tired. Why don't you take a nap, while I phone Bianca? You're going to be up again most of the night."

Valentino shot her a glance. "We'll take a rest together." They'd done the same thing yesterday. It had been heaven. "No matter how well you've felt today, you need some downtime, too."

"I confess that sounds good."

They left the kitchen and headed into the bedroom where both of them took off their shoes and stretched out across the top of the quilt. "Here. Use my phone."

"Thank you." She took it from him and called her family's home number. Her mother answered.

"Clara? I heard you came by yesterday."

"We were sorry to miss you, Mamma. How's Bianca?"

"She's resting right now, but she's going to be fine."

"The poor thing. She needs to get a lot of sleep."

"We'll see to it. Don't you worry about anything."

She glanced at her husband, whose eyes were closed. "Tino won't let me. He keeps me too busy to think."

"That's good."

"Guess what I did today?" For the next five minutes she related the experience driving his car.

Her mother gasped several times. "You could have gotten both of you killed!"

Ever since the police had pulled her over, Clara had been regretting her impulsive behavior. If anything had happened to Valentino because of her...

"I won't ever speed again, Mamma."

With those words Valentino's arm caught her around the hips. "Promise me," he whispered.

She'd thought he'd fallen asleep. "I promise."

"What did you say, Clara?"

"I'm sorry, Mamma. I was just answering Tino."

"I can tell you've had a good day."

"A wonderful day."

"That makes me happy."

"Me, too."

"I'll talk to you soon."

"*Ciao*, Mamma."

The minute she hung up, Valentino pulled her closer. "Let me hold you like this for a while."

She made a little moan of consent and nestled against him with her head lying on his shoulder. If they both slept now, she would read her mystery tonight. They used to read to each other when they had literature assignments. Maybe he'd like her to read aloud to him. They could hash over the plot. She'd lived for their lively discussions. He had the most fascinating mind...

No one knew how much she'd missed him over the years. To have him back in her life like this constituted some kind of miracle. As her eyes closed her hand slid to his chest without conscious thought.

She had no idea how long she slept, but when she was once again cognizant of her surroundings it surprised her that she and Valentino had changed positions. While she lay on her side, he was now turned toward her with his head buried in her neck. His hand roved over her back in ever tightening circles, wringing tiny sounds of pleasure from her throat.

When his mouth found hers, it seemed natural to indulge in a giving and taking that grew more sensual with each breath. "I love the taste of you. Your body feels made for mine." He drew in a deep breath. "I want to make love to you, Clara. Is it selfish of me to want you so badly?"

Her breath caught. He wanted her. "How could it be selfish? I don't understand what you mean?"

"Would it make you feel worse?"

Worse— "I've never felt better, but if you're asking me for health reasons, I couldn't honestly tell you how it would affect me," she whispered against his lips, unable to get enough of them. "My body seems to dissolve a little more with every kiss." She didn't want to talk right now.

"Have you ever been intimate with a man before?"

"Not like this," she murmured, thrilling to each caress.

Maybe it was her imagination but she thought she heard him groan. "Has your doctor given you any guidelines?"

"No. The subject never came up. Does it matter?" She tried to get closer to him. "I don't want you to stop kissing me."

His hands stilled on her arms. "That's my fear—that I won't be able to stop." His breathing sounded shallow.

"Would that be so terrible?" she asked, kissing him more passionately.

"Considering your condition, it would be unconscionable if I got you pregnant, *piccola*. Even the best protection isn't completely safe."

While she was digesting the long-term ramifications, he untangled his legs from hers and rolled out of reach. When he stood up, she couldn't bear it. All her joy evaporated. "Please come back to bed. We'll just hold each other for the rest of the night."

He shook his dark head, taking another step away from her. "I'm afraid not. Carlo will be pulling up in the drive any moment."

Carlo. She'd forgotten all about his coming again. Valentino had taken her to another world. If the clinician were to walk in right now, he'd find her a throbbing mass of needs her husband had aroused. She couldn't imagine getting to sleep. If he refused to touch her from now on, it would be like a second death.

CHAPTER NINE

WHEN Clara awakened early Saturday morning and opened her eyes, she saw that Valentino was already up and dressed in a pullover and jeans. Normally he slept in until ten to catch up on his sleep. During those hours she would get out of bed and leave him alone while she followed through with her own routine. Deprivation was one sure form of self-preservation.

However this morning there was an air of expectancy about him. When he was up to something, he couldn't hide it from her. She loved that quality about him. In truth she loved all his qualities, which were too numerous to count.

Valentino took amazing care of her. What little she did for him by being a listening ear when he chose to divulge his inner thoughts could never make up for the hours he watched over her while administering her treatments. During those hours while she slept, he balanced his time between helping her and running his business from the laptop.

After six consecutive nights of dialysis she felt so normal, she had a hard time believing there was anything wrong with her.

His dark eyes swept over her face and hair. "If you feel as good as you look, I've arranged a surprise for you."

She got excited because his surprises weren't like anyone else's. Every day they went out on the scooter to explore neighboring villages and enjoy picnics. They traveled to all their old haunts and sought new ones, finding delight in everything they did.

But with each passing hour, her physical attraction to him was growing more intense. The only time she could legitimately touch him without worrying what he might think was when she clung to him on the back of his scooter.

He represented the epitome of male sensuality and could have no idea that each time he squeezed or kissed her coming and going he added to the fire raging inside her. If he thought they could go on this way indefinitely, then he truly didn't know how deeply her desire burned for him.

Despite the fact that she was ill, the nature of their relationship would have led to intimacy by now *if* they were in a normal marriage. But they weren't! Valentino needed her as a friend. Though he was a flesh and blood male with the normal urges, he'd been careful not to let things go too far.

She, on the other hand, had to fight not to reveal that a little friendly loving was slowly destroying her.

Feeling his gaze on her, she said, "Judging by the way you're dressed, we're doing some kind of activity outside. Shall I wear my leather jacket?"

"I think you'll prefer a parka, but bring your gloves. I'll meet you out in the kitchen in a few minutes."

Within twenty they'd eaten breakfast and had stolen away from the villa in the Ferrari. Dawn still lay over Monta Correnti. Clara had always considered it a magical time of day when there was a crispness in the air and all was quiet. Valentino must have been enchanted, too, because he didn't talk. They wound their way past the church where the road made a descent and disappeared into the picture-book countryside.

She didn't understand when he eventually turned off onto a

dirt road bordered by well-tended farms. Maybe he'd found another property for sale he wanted to show her.

Ahead of them she saw a van pulled to the side. A couple of men were walking around carrying items. "Uh oh. They must have had car trouble."

"Let's find out," Valentino murmured. He pulled to a stop behind them and got out of the car.

Clara craned her neck to find out what was going on and got the shock of her life to see them unraveling a huge balloon over the ground. A thrill of excitement tinged with alarm shot through her. Valentino had arranged to take them for a balloon ride?

Once she'd extricated herself from the seat harness, she joined him. The men, a father and son, greeted her with broad smiles. Evidently they were good friends of Valentino's. He introduced everyone.

"*Buon giorno, signora*. You have chosen the perfect morning to go up."

Valentino's gaze flicked to hers. She saw a definite look of concern in those dark brown depths. "What do you think, *piccola*? Do you want to try it?" He didn't ask how she was feeling, but she knew he was worried.

Clara had never been on a plane, let alone anything that had ever left the ground. But this was Valentino Casali who'd established a record for the longest solo balloon flight over the Caribbean. She didn't want to let him down and would show him and his friends that daredevil side he'd accused her of having when she'd driven his Ferrari for the first time.

"I'm dying to find out what it's like!"

Her unintentional slip of the tongue washed over the men, who got busy inflating the balloon, but she saw Valentino's lips tighten for a moment before he moved behind her and slid his hands to her shoulders.

He kneaded them with increasing pressure. "As I've told you several times, you're a woman of great courage, but this is one time when you have to be completely honest with me, or we won't step foot inside the basket."

She took a fortifying breath. "Physically I feel fine, but I'll admit to being scared."

He kissed the side of her neck, sending rivulets of yearning through her body. "That's natural. At first it will feel like you're in a lift that doesn't stop. Then you'll float over a world only the eagle sees. You'll be so full of wonder, you'll never want to come down. I'll have hold of you every second."

Whatever happened, if she could remain in his arms like this, nothing else mattered.

The multicolored balloon straightened as the men filled it with hot air. Valentino knew when the moment was right and helped her into the basket. "While his father is in charge, Agostino will follow our progress in the van. When we descend, he'll drive us back here."

She nodded and clung to him.

In a few minutes he whispered, "Clara?" There was a sense of urgency in his tone that caused her to lift her head. Maybe it was a trick of light, but she thought she glimpsed the heat of desire in his eyes before his mouth covered hers. The moment he deepened their kiss, she forgot where she was or what was happening around them.

Not even she could mistake the force he was unleashing as anything less than a husband's kiss. She'd been needing this for so long, her hunger for him took over and her passion flared. It would have been impossible to hold back even if she'd wanted to for propriety's sake. She had so much to tell him, show him. At this point nothing but a total merging of their bodies would satisfy her.

In the throes of rapture she cried his name with longing.

He drew one more molten kiss from her mouth before he said, "We're up now. Take a look."

She could hardly make sense of what he was saying until she opened her eyes. Then a gasp flew out of her. "Tino—"

They were airborne!

Clara had missed the ascent because she'd been devouring her husband in front of his friend with an eagerness that made her blush scarlet just thinking about it.

Valentino kept her clamped at his side while she marveled at the vista unfolding several thousand feet below. She'd never seen such a sight, let alone experienced a sensation like it.

"I feel like we're fruit blossoms being carried along by the breeze."

He folded her right up against him and kissed her hard. "You feel a little more substantial to me than that. I wish there weren't so many clothes separating us."

The unexpected admission rang of need rather than playfulness, robbing her of breath. This was the passionate side of Valentino he'd revealed before he'd had the presence of mind to end what was rapidly burning out of control.

In a moment of truth she confessed, "I had the same thought." For the next half-hour she kept her hot face buried in his neck. They passed over the fantastic tapestry best seen from this altitude, but Valentino had just unlocked a door to her own private fantasies.

At the height of her euphoria, sharp searing pain, bitter and real, attacked without warning. Please, God. I don't want to die.

He kissed her hair, increasing her agony. "What did you say, *piccola*?"

"Th-that I wish this day could go on forever," she dissembled in a tremulous voice.

"Why can't it? When we get back, how would you like to drive to Monaco? We'll stay for a few days. I'll take you to the track where we practice. I want to show off my gorgeous wife to the team. I love this new life with you, Clara."

I love it, too, her soul cried out in fresh anguish. Maybe it was wishful thinking on her part, but Valentino *did* seem happier lately, more relaxed. It couldn't all be an act, could it? Not after they'd come close to making love—unless he was carrying his husbandly duty to the extreme.

She'd lived with him long enough to know he was capable of doing anything to make life more enjoyable for her. Knowing her days were numbered, would he go that far? To add to her torment, Silvio's silent questions kept flashing through her mind.

Is he in love with you, Clara? Did he say those words to you? Because if he didn't…

They landed without incident in the middle of another country road. The van was waiting there to take them back to their car. She shook the men's hands. "*Grazie, signori*. It was *stupendo*."

On the return trip to the villa Valentino said, "While you pack, I'll go by the restaurant and talk to Papa and Isabella so they know our plans."

Clara nodded. "Would you like me to put some things in a suitcase for you?"

He kissed the end of her nose. "I'd like that very much. So far there's nothing about our marriage that doesn't make me happy. I can't think why I waited so long. Do you have any complaints?"

"Except for the fact that you fish for compliments when you don't need to, you know I don't. Thank you for another wonderful experience I'll never forget." On that note she leaned over to peck his jaw, then got out of the car and hurried inside the villa to get ready for their trip.

Unless something unforeseen happened, she wasn't going to die today, tomorrow, or even next week. That meant she should make the most of living on the borrowed time dialysis was granting her.

When they reached Monaco, she would forget her illness and love Valentino in all the ways he would allow her. If they both used protection, there would be no worry about her getting pregnant.

Clara had loved him her whole life, but today she realized she was a woman *in love*. She couldn't go back to their platonic relationship. Not now. It wasn't possible.

On the way to the restaurant Valentino's thoughts were on Clara and the way she'd clung to him during their balloon ride. She wanted him as much as he wanted her. For purely selfish reasons this countdown needed to come to an end.

He reached for his phone to let his sister know he was coming, but realized he'd left it on the dresser back at the villa. It didn't matter. When he parked out back and joined Isabella upstairs, he found her still in the apartment making breakfast for their father. The timing was perfect. Valentino could eat with him while she went to market.

As he entered the kitchen it struck him how warm and colorful she'd made the apartment. The place looked lived in and comfortable, the antithesis of his villa in Monaco as well as the one he was living in now. He discovered he couldn't wait to move into his own farmhouse with Clara.

On top of the upright piano in the corner his sister had put photographs of their mother and the family. He wandered over to it and studied the likeness of her he remembered best. Because of a certain conversation with Clara, his stomach didn't clench as it usually did. His wife had changed him so much already, he didn't know himself.

"Izzy?" He headed into the dining room where she'd set the table. "I'm taking Clara to Monaco with me for a couple of days. I have to meet with my sponsor. He knows I've quit racing, but I'd like to tell him in person."

"Is she well enough to travel?"

"The nightly dialysis has made a new woman of her."

Her eyes watered. "I'm so glad, but waiting for a kidney must be so hard on both of you."

"We've been doing our best not to think about it." Valentino didn't tell her that he was waiting for a phone call from Dr. Arno with the results of his own tests.

"Trust me to bring it up."

He gave her a hug. "Thank you for caring so much. I didn't want to leave town without telling you and let you think I was deserting you again."

She shook her head. "I wouldn't think that, but I'm glad you're here. Papa's been asking about you. I'll get him."

"Let me do it," he interjected. "You go. I'll take care of him until you get back."

"Thanks. I realize you're anxious to get going so I won't be more than a half-hour."

"Perfect."

Once she was out the door, he walked down the hall and knocked on his father's bedroom door. "Papa?"

"Is that you, Valentino?"

He always said that, even though he knew who it was on the other side. "Who else? I came to eat breakfast with you."

"Ah—I'm coming."

"Don't forget your cane."

"No one will let me forget it!" he grumbled as he emerged in his tan trousers and matching sport shirt. His eyes stared at Valentino. "How is your Clara?"

"Good, all things considered."

His father's progress was slow. They finally reached the dining room and sat down at the table where Isabella had left warm rolls, fruit and cappuccino. Valentino helped adjust the chair for him and rested his cane against the table leg.

"She's a brave woman. Noble, too."

"That's an interesting choice of words, Papa." Valentino had thought the same thing about her, but didn't expect to hear his father express it.

"Well, isn't she? The way she carries on with that sunny disposition makes me ashamed of the way I've been complaining." He cleared his throat. "While we're alone, I want to tell you how proud I am of you for taking such good care of her."

Valentino sensed his father's sincerity. Another surprise. "Aunt Lisa asked me if I had lost my mind."

"When did she dare talk to you?"

"She phoned me the other night while I was giving Clara a treatment."

His father munched on his roll for a minute. "My sister is a born troublemaker. I happen to know you had a special feeling for the Rossetti girl from the time your poor mamma died. Listen to me, my son, because you *are* my son, even if you aren't my blood."

Valentino lifted his head to stare at this man he thought he knew.

"I can see what a terrible mistake I made by not adopting you years ago, but I was afraid."

"Of what?" Valentino whispered in shock. He couldn't believe they were having this conversation.

To his surprise, Luca's eyes watered. "I was such a failure as a father to my first two sons, I didn't feel I had the right to claim you for my own. Violetta didn't dare talk to me about it. With hindsight I can see she felt so guilty for the affair, she was afraid to ask me. But I was to blame for much of the trouble during that period. Earning a living was always a struggle. It caused difficulties in both my marriages."

In the silence that followed, his father wept quietly. "I didn't feel worthy of the honor to be your father officially."

Valentino lowered his head, unable to talk. Emotion had closed up his throat.

"I don't expect you to understand how it was for me as a

young man. I fell for the twins' mother, but she wasn't happy here in Italy. She was an exciting, glamorous American woman who had a high-powered and glamorous job to match. But she didn't feel accepted here and when our twins were born, her partying had to come to an end.

"I was struggling to keep my roadside stall running. Things just didn't work out. When the children turned two, she left them with me and went back to Boston where she divorced me."

"What?" Valentino was incredulous. "From the way Aunt Lisa made it sound, you abandoned them."

"That didn't come until later." Sorrow twisted his features. "My business didn't make any money. By the time the children turned three, I was in desperate financial trouble and asked Lisa for a loan just to buy the boys some food until the situation improved. Sorella was doing well and I promised I would pay her back with interest if she would just help me out for a while."

Valentino could already see the writing on the wall. "She didn't lend you any money, did she?"

"No. Not that she had to, but I had no one else to turn to. She told me I ought to send the boys to their mother in Boston since she had a lot more money and could take care of them properly."

It was always the money with Valentino's aunt, yet she'd never told anyone she'd turned down his father's request for a loan.

His father took a shuddering breath. "I was in dire straits, Valentino. I loved my boys more than you can imagine, but I was unable to provide for them at the time. In the end I had no choice but to send them to their mother. It was the hardest thing I ever had to do, especially when I never knew my own father."

The similarity of Luca's and Valentino's beginnings wasn't wasted on him.

"Don't get me wrong. I'm not making excuses. I'm only trying to give you an explanation for the reason I never told you children about the twins. I was too ashamed over my inability to provide for them. It took me years to start earning enough money to be a family man."

More tears trickled down. "I don't expect forgiveness from anyone. I called the boys on their eighteenth birthdays. They didn't want anything to do with me. Who could blame them?" He put up his hand. "But before you leave here today, I want you to know something.

"When you were born, I named you Valentino in honor of my father, William Valentine. Besides my love, it was the most precious thing I could give you. Your mamma wanted that name for you, too."

The revelations just kept coming.

"How she loved her Tino. The diabetes she suffered from was a terrible disease. With every blackout I feared it was the end and you children would lose your mother."

Valentino's breath caught. "*Every* blackout? You mean it happened more than once?"

"Yes, but we didn't tell you so you wouldn't get alarmed. The doctor said she was dead before she fell down the stairs. Cristiano was just old enough to feel guilty that he hadn't gotten home sooner that day."

"I felt guilty, too, and thought I was to blame because I couldn't revive her."

A heavy sigh escaped. "How sad that both my sons took on that extra burden when you were already suffering."

Clara had been right.

While his mind grappled with information that cleared up the distorted picture he'd carried around for years, they heard Isabella enter the apartment. "I'm back, in case anyone wants to know!"

"Come and join us!" their father called out.

"In a moment."

Valentino eyed him through new eyes. "Papa?"

"Yes?"

"I don't want you to worry about finances anymore. If you don't like my ideas for increasing the business, I'd like to make you a loan to help pay off any debts you have owing because I know you'll pay it back when you can."

His father resisted.

"Let me do this for you. If you hadn't given me a good life, I wouldn't be in the position I am now. Think about it and we'll talk again after Clara and I get back from Monaco in a couple of days."

He patted his arm. "I'm overwhelmed, but you need to keep it for your family now."

"There's enough to do both." Valentino got to his feet, eager to get back to his wife. He had so much to tell her, it would take the whole drive to Monaco. Only a few more days! Surely Dr. Arno would call any day with the results of Valentino's tests and Clara's transplant could go ahead. Then their lives would truly begin…

Clara had just hung up from talking to her mother to tell her their plans when she heard Valentino's cell phone ring. He'd obviously gone off without it. She lifted it from the dresser to glance at the caller ID, assuming it was someone from his company.

To her surprise it was coming from the Immaculata Teaching Hospital in Rome. Her body shook in reaction. She wondered what it could mean. Dr. Arno's office was there.

She clicked on. "*Pronto*?"

"Signor Casali, *per favore*."

"He's not here, but this is his wife Signora Casali. May I take a message for him?"

No sooner had she said it than her husband walked in their bedroom, his dark eyes searching out her gaze.

"This is the lab calling from Immaculata Hospital in Rome. Your husband asked that he be notified the minute his test results were done. Please tell him they've been sent to Dr. Arno's office."

The person on the other end gave out a phone number before the line went dead, but Clara's mind was reeling.

She stared at Valentino. "That was the hospital in Rome letting you know Dr. Arno had the results of your tests. They must have you mixed up with me, but before I could question it, they hung up. You'd better call them back."

As she handed it to him her cell phone rang. It was still lying on the bed. She reached for it and said hello.

"Clara?"

The familiar voice caused her heart to thud. "Hello, Dr. Arno." Was he calling because the blood Carlo had drawn the other night showed her anemia was worse?

"It's good to hear your voice. How are you doing on the nightly dialysis?"

"Fine. I've been feeling better and better," she said while Valentino stood there watching her in a way that raised the hairs on the back of her neck.

"That's wonderful." After a distinct pause he said, "I have even more wonderful news for you."

As she continued to look at Valentino, pure revelation flowed through her. "You mean about my husband volunteering a kidney for me?" A softness had entered his eyes, too piercingly sweet for her to sustain. She turned away from him.

"Then Valentino told you. We both felt it would be better if the identity of your donor remained a secret until you came into the hospital for the transplant, but as long as you already know…"

Clara bowed her head, praying for the inspiration to make it through this phone call. "To say I'm in shock would be putting it mildly." All this time he'd been laying the ground-work… The extent of his self-sacrifice staggered her.

"The *best* kind of shock there is. You both need to check in the hospital as soon as you can get here."

"You're talking today?" The rhetorical question came out more for herself than for him.

"Preferably in the next two hours so the lab can run a few more tests on you. If all looks good, we'll do the transplant in the morning."

By now Valentino had walked around so she was forced to look at him. Clara closed her eyes tightly.

"I'm afraid we won't be coming, Dr. Arno."

"I don't understand."

"You see, we're on our way to Monaco for a few days so Valentino can talk to his sponsor face to face. He's already turned his home into a hospital and has given up his racing career for me. I won't allow him to give up one of his kidneys, too." Scalding tears ran their course down her cheeks. "That's carrying altruism to an extreme not even God would condone."

"*Piccola—*"

The endearment scorched her to the depths of her soul. She turned away from him again. "Please don't give up searching for a viable donor, Dr. Arno. I know *I* won't."

After hanging up, she walked into the bathroom to wash the moisture from her cheeks. When she came out again, an ashen-faced Valentino was still standing where she'd left him.

"I'm ready to leave for Monaco whenever you are. Our bags are packed."

His features looked chiseled. "We're driving to Rome."

An unnatural calm had come over her. "Father Orsini gave us one charge. To make the other person happy. It would make me very happy to see where you used to live. I'd like to meet your racing buddies. You have no idea how much I've looked forward to this trip."

He studied her for a long time. "We just got married. I don't want you to die. My idea of happiness trumps yours."

Valentino had a way with words and arguments that had always twisted her emotions until she was defeated, but not this time. "Not if it means your death, and it could… I'm not simply referring to the risk you take for undergoing an operation. There's the rest of your life to consider. If it were shortened because of this experience, I couldn't handle that along with everything else on my conscience."

"Then let me remind you of something Dr. Arno told me."

Clara saw the compassion in his eyes. It was too much. "I don't want to hear it."

She grabbed her purse and phone, then reached for her suitcase and started out of the bedroom. He followed with the bag she'd packed for him.

"You'll like it," he persisted after they'd reached the kitchen. "To quote him, 'At times like these, I always tell my patients to be thankful to God. In his wisdom, he gave everyone two kidneys, even though he knew we only needed one. That's so we could give the other one away.'"

She spun around. "I'm sorry, but that lovely little story doesn't make me feel better."

"It should," he fired back. "I don't need both of mine. By this time tomorrow you'll have a functioning kidney again. In four to five more days we'll be home from the hospital. With the medication he plans for you to take to minimize your body's rejection, you'll be ready to throw yourself into the limoncello business before you know it."

She lowered her suitcase to the floor. "The day could come when one of your kidneys won't work. Then you'll be thankful you still have the other one."

"If that moment should come, then I'll find me a donor."

He always had an answer. "What's the real reason for all this?" she demanded.

His eyes glittered. "The real reason? That covers a lot of territory, but I suppose it was something Father Orsini said that played into it."

Clara didn't know if she could tolerate hearing it, but she needed to know the whole truth now. "What was it?"

"He told me you could use a friend."

"I wish he hadn't said anything."

"How could he not? You're a favorite with everyone."

"That's not true," she cried softly.

"It's pointless to argue the fact. Needless to say his remark shot straight to my gut because I realized you'd always been my one abiding friend, the one person who continually built me up and made me believe in myself without asking anything in return."

The surprising explanation knocked the foundation out from under her.

Valentino moved closer. "I thought about it all the way back to the villa. You were the only reason my visit to Monta Correnti had sounded palatable. You know what happened when we saw each other on the stairs."

Yes. She knew. Her body trembled just remembering how he hadn't left her alone since.

"When I followed you to the clinic, I finally had a way to give you back something of myself for a change."

She felt her limbs dissolve when his hands slid to her shoulders. "You know me," he said in a husky tone. "I don't believe in what I can't see, but if my kidney could make you well, it would probably change my mind for me. Will you at least think about it while we're in Monaco?"

Once again he'd confounded her as only he could do. But even if he'd made her heart bleed, she would never let him go through that for her.

"Yes," she muttered. "Now can we please go?" She eased away, forcing him to relinquish his hold of her.

He carried their cases out the door and put them in the car

before helping her in the passenger side. "I'll be back with the machine."

In a few minutes they were ready and left the grounds. The gate closed behind them. "I've never been to the Costa Azzurra or Monaco."

"We'll stop several times along the way to eat and stretch so the drive won't be too much for you."

"Thank you." He never stopped thinking about her comfort for a second. "How close is your villa to the place where you drove in the Grand Prix?"

"Mine overlooks the main street."

"I know your sponsor has tapes, but it's sad you never got to stand on your own balcony and see yourself driving."

He broke into that male laughter she loved so much. "You're priceless, you know that? Wait till I tell the guys."

"At least you never crashed there."

"How do you know that?" His glance lingered on her profile.

"Bianca and I watched your races and saw every crash you were in." Each time she had almost died from fear.

"I didn't realize that," came the solemn admission. He reached out and grasped her hand to kiss it before letting it go again.

"It's a miracle you're still alive."

"Dr. Rimbaud told me the same thing every time he patched me back together."

She took a shaky breath. "Thank you for taking me on this trip."

"I've been looking forward to it, too, *piccola*."

"Even if there are other things you need to be doing?"

"Like what?" he demanded. "I'm your husband. This is where I need to be."

"I'm the most pampered wife I know." She was still so shaken by his plan to give her a kidney, she couldn't keep the tears out of her voice. "I loved this morning's balloon ride. How lucky was I to have the whole world at my feet?"

"I won't forget it either."

Her emotions were all over the place. "Tell me how it went with your father earlier, or didn't you get to see him?"

He let out a deep sigh. "He was there. Thanks to you, this morning we talked like we've never talked in our lives."

It was clear something monumental had happened. Without forethought she clutched his hard-muscled arm for a moment. "That's good."

"You have no idea."

Clara turned so she could watch him while he drove. She would never grow tired of looking at him. In profile or other-wise, his masculine beauty was stunning. "I want to hear all about it. Don't leave anything out."

Late afternoon of the following day, Valentino left his sponsor's office and walked out to the practice track. It surprised him the sun felt this hot. He was glad for it since he knew Clara welcomed the warmth.

He spotted half a dozen racers on his team surrounding his green-eyed wife seated in the middle of the bleachers. For the occasion she'd worn a wispy, periwinkle-colored blouse and white wraparound skirt with matching Italian sandals. Every color suited her.

Clara's knockout looks were only superseded by a feminine charm that came from someone grateful for life and interested in everyone. She projected that rare selflessness, guaranteed to melt the most cynical heart.

"So, Signora Casali?" He loved calling her that. It was a supreme moment for him to introduce her as his wife. When all this was a new experience for her, he was proud of her and the way she handled herself. "Are the guys giving you a hard time?"

"Oh, no." She flashed him one of her mysterious smiles.

"They've been entertaining me with unabridged stories about you." Jocular laughter ensued.

Roger, a three-time world Formula 1 champion, grinned at him, giving him the thumbs-up sign. "Your *belle épouse* has so many statistics in her head, she could write her own book on you. I'm jealous, *mon ami*. You have found yourself a *trésor*."

Valentino agreed with him and nodded before looking around. Most of the journalists who'd come to the track for a photo shoot had gone, but there were still a few left who'd been waiting to get last-minute pictures of him and Clara. They never gave up. Today had been his swan song.

Normally he would have hated the invasion of privacy, but having his wife with him made all the difference. He no longer felt defensive or uptight. In fact the cameramen scarcely impinged on his consciousness.

Pleased that she seemed to be taking it in her stride, he climbed the bleachers two at a time to hunker down behind her and put his arms around her neck. He kissed her tender nape where she smelled of flowers from her lotion. "What do you say we leave and enjoy dinner on the water?"

He felt the little tremor that ran through her body before she whispered, "I'd love it."

A few more pictures while he helped her off the bleachers and they headed for his car. Once inside, he drove them down the zigzag streets of Monaco City to the yacht harbor. Hand in hand they strolled toward the Quai des Savants. This was a local paparazzi hangout, but tonight he didn't care. "I thought you'd enjoy eating at a modern Parisian-style bistro."

The reflected lights off the water from the yachts created an illusion that her eyes were dancing. After they were seated, she smiled at him. "I don't speak French. You order for us."

"They serve a delicious veal escalope with mushroom sauce. I like a Madeira wine with it."

"It all sounds delicious, but will you tell them to leave the sauce off mine in case there's some dairy in it?"

He'd already anticipated doing it. After the waiter left with their order, Valentino got to his feet. "Let's dance."

"I haven't done it for a long time."

Once he'd pulled her from the chair, he drew her into his arms. "That excuse might have worked years ago, but you're my wife now. I don't care if you can't." He smiled down at her. "We'll just stand here and hold each other."

"Tino—"

He loved it when she blushed. While he was enjoying the moment, and her, and the night, she blew him away with some fantastic moves. They got lost in the music. He couldn't remember ever having this much fun dancing or anything else.

"Don't look now, but our dinner's waiting for us," she reminded him.

With reluctance, he guided her back to their table. "Next time, don't be so modest. You're a sensational dancer."

"Bianca and I used to practice."

Unable to resist, he pressed a kiss to her unsuspecting lips before seating her.

It didn't take long before she moaned. "I can't eat another bite."

"No dessert?"

She shook her head. "But don't let me stop you."

He had no intention of allowing that to happen, but the time wasn't yet...

As soon as they returned to the car, he took her past the Grimaldi Palace. At her request, he drove them around the Grand Prix racing circuit. She expressed a desire to visit the casino. He told her they'd do more sightseeing tomorrow. Though her energy seemed limitless, Valentino knew she had to be exhausted and finally pulled into the back of his empire-style villa for the night.

She hurried to their bedroom and got ready for bed fast.

"With you having to be up for my treatment tonight, we shouldn't have stayed out so late, Tino."

"I wanted to. We'll both sleep in tomorrow."

True to what she'd told him on their wedding night, she fell asleep within thirty seconds of her head touching the pillow. It worried him she'd overextended herself. He'd be more careful with her from now on. Unfortunately when she'd refused to go to Rome with him he'd been forced to pull out all the stops to get their marriage back on the right track.

For the last eight hours he'd purposely avoided any talk of kidney donors or her illness. His strategy had paid off. Tonight Clara had acted more relaxed and confident with him than he'd ever seen her.

Little by little they were settling into their marriage. From the moment he'd approached her parents, it had shocked him how right it had felt.

Once Valentino got her treatment started for the night, he pulled out his laptop. A dozen e-mails from Violetta Rapidita had been sent and needed replies. Isabella had written him, too. He opened it, wondering if this was bad news about their father.

Fratello mio, I didn't know how long you'd be in Monaco. In case you decided to stay there longer with Clara, I thought I'd better tell you what's happening. I don't want you to come back to Monta Correnti and be surprised in case you should run into Lizzie or Aunt Lisa and hear something you weren't aware of.

First off you need to know Lizzie and I have made up because we absolutely hate this war between Papa and Aunt Lisa. More than anything Papa wants the family to be reunited and we're in agreement.

Since the two of you talked the other day, he said he's done with secrets. After regretting that he kept quiet about the twins, he's told the cousins you're not his birth son, but he loves you as if you were. He doesn't want anyone hurting you later on.

Valentino rubbed a hand over his face.

Secondly, I know you're upset with me for getting in contact with the twins, but how can our family ever come together if things remain as they are? As you know, Lizzie and Jack are planning a June wedding, so she has sent invitations to Angelo and Alessandro.

The amazing twins were coming?

She's hoping everyone will show up. I do, too. Please don't be angry with me about this. Life's too short, don't you think?
Talk to you when you get back.
Love, Izzy

The penultimate line gave him pause because he found he couldn't disagree with his sister. Life *was* too short where Clara was concerned. Compared to doing everything to keep her alive, all else paled in significance, even his family's problems.

He stared into space. Before he answered his sister and told her his plans, he needed to send an e-mail to Dr. Arno, who deserved an explanation. The situation was bordering on desperate.

CHAPTER TEN

A WEEK later Clara drove to the farm early to spend the day with her family. She'd left her husband sleeping.

Since the morning she'd told Valentino she wouldn't let him give her a kidney, she'd noticed an alarming change in their relationship. It seemed that her refusal had killed his desire for the little amount of intimacy they'd shared.

On the surface he was the model husband and still affectionate with her, but in bed he didn't even try to hold her anymore. His behavior went beyond his fear that he might make her pregnant. They could have worked around that. To her sorrow he didn't leave himself open to discussion of their situation. For that matter he avoided any talk of her medical condition.

Since their return from Monaco, she'd had one conversation with Dr. Arno. He'd been understanding of the reasons she couldn't let Valentino be a donor, and he'd assured her everything was being done to find her one. Clara was trying to stay positive and stopped by the clinic for routine blood checks.

Because of Valentino's devoted service to her, he'd made it possible for her to lead what seemed like a normal life, but she was terrified he wasn't getting anything out of it. Not even a saint could go on like this much longer. Neither could she…

It all came down to one reality. Her husband was the source

of her joy and her pain, and this dichotomy of emotions was tearing her apart.

"I think you need to confront him," Bianca advised her some time later while she let Clara bathe Paolito. Her poor sister was still suffering horrible morning sickness. Until the advent of her nightly dialysis, Clara had lived with nausea and wouldn't wish it on her worst enemy.

She splashed water on the baby, who could sit up in the water if she propped him. "Any suggestions on how to do it?"

"Yes. When you drive back to town, buy yourself something sexy from that little lingerie shop on the Via Romana. Something black and filmy. You're gorgeous in black. Tomorrow morning fix your hair different and put on a different perfume. Be lying there next to him when he wakes up. Tell him it's time he had a treatment from you, then do what comes naturally."

Clara swallowed hard. "Then he'll know."

"You mean that you're madly in love with him?"

As she nodded their mother came in the bathroom. "Your cell phone rang while I was in the kitchen, Clara. I'll take over here with Paolito while you find out if it was important. If it's Valentino, tell him to come for dinner. I'm making his favorite cannelloni."

Clara and her sister shared a secret smile. "I'll tell him," she assured her mamma before hurrying downstairs. Just the thought that it might be her husband caused her heart to thud in anticipation.

She reached for her purse lying on the table and pulled out her phone to check the caller ID. It threw her off balance to discover Dr. Arno had phoned. He'd left a voice message.

"Clara? You need to come to the hospital as fast as you can. A kidney is suddenly available. Don't eat or drink anything. The nursing staff will alert me as soon as you've checked in and we'll go from there."

With hands trembling, she phoned Valentino. Pick up, Tino. Please pick up!

"*Piccola*?" he answered on the third ring. "Are you all right?" The concern in his voice was always there. How she loved him!

"Yes! Where are you?" she blurted.

"Getting ready to walk down to the restaurant. Why?"

"I'm coming for you. We have to drive to Rome immediately. I've got a donor!"

After a pregnant pause, "*Grazie a Dio*." His voice throbbed. "I'll pack a bag for you and meet you below the gate. Whatever you do, don't have an accident on the way. My heart couldn't handle it."

Neither could hers. "I won't." Her voice shook. After she hung up, she shouted, "Mamma?"

"I'm right behind you and heard everything. Someone must have died, making it possible for my precious Clara to live." She wept. "Go, *bambina*! Every second counts! Your father and I will come to the hospital as soon as we can."

Whoever it was had to have signed a donor card while they were still living. As far as Clara was concerned, they were part angel.

Six hours later one of the nurses walked in Clara's hospital room. "They're ready for you, Signora Casali. You have two minutes before they come with the gurney to wheel you to the OR."

Clara nodded, overcome by the outpouring of love from her family. All the adults were here, gathered around her bed. Silvio hadn't left her side since his arrival with Maria. For once he didn't show his resentment of Valentino, which was a blessing in itself.

After her father kissed her one last time, her gaze finally fastened on her dashing husband, whose brown eyes were suspiciously bright.

He squeezed her hand. "This is it, my brave Clarissima."

"Oh, Tino—"

"I'll be with you every step of the way."

"I know that," she whispered in a tremulous voice.

"When you wake up, it will be to a new life." He lowered his mouth to hers in a kiss that felt more like a benediction than husbandly.

A new fear tore at her heart as she was wheeled out of the room.

The minute Clara was gone, Valentino turned to her family. "Dr. Arno says none of us can expect to see or talk to her until at least ten or eleven o'clock tonight. Do whatever you want until then. I'll be here the whole time and plan to catch up on some sleep while I wait."

Clara's mother hugged him. "You do that. No one deserves it more. We will see you tonight."

Once they'd all left the floor, he stepped across the hall to another room prepared for him where he quickly removed his clothes and put on a hospital gown. After he got in bed, a team of medical staff came in to prep him. Soon he was being wheeled out the door and down the hall to the OR.

Throughout his racing career he'd faced surgery several times for a bone to be set, but this was different. He loved the idea that one of his kidneys would be planted inside Clara. They'd had a connection since childhood. With this transplant, that connection would be indelible. Personal. Life-giving. Eternal. Belonging only to the two of them.

One day soon he hoped to plant something else inside her enticing body that would result in bringing both of them ineffable joy.

Clara kept waking up. Each time she did, she became more aware of her surroundings. Where was Valentino?

The next time she opened her eyes, she realized she was

back in a different room with a new nurse who was taking her vital signs.

"It's good to see you awake, Signora Casali."

"What time is it?"

"Midnight. You're in the transplant unit."

"I can't believe nine hours have passed."

"How are you feeling?"

"Strange."

"Strange is good."

"Where's my husband?"

"In time you'll be able to see everyone. Relax right now. Let the drugs do their job."

Between the anesthetic and other drugs being fed through the IV, she was feeling no pain, but the sight of the big machine next to her bed alarmed her.

"Did something go wrong with the transplant?"

The middle-aged woman smiled. "Don't you remember Dr. Arno telling you it went perfectly?"

"He did? Then why is the dialysis machine here?"

"In case your new kidney doesn't function right away. You probably don't remember him explaining that to you either." She gave Clara some pills to swallow. "Just take a few small sips."

"The water tastes good."

"Tomorrow you'll be able to drink liquids. Depending on how you're feeling, you'll probably be able to eat a little bit, too. Do you have any questions for me?"

"No, but I would like to see my husband."

"Tell you what. I'll go back to the desk and see how soon a visit is allowed."

"Thank you."

Before long she heard a familiar voice say her name. She opened her eyes. "Hi, Dr. Arno. The nurse told me everything went well."

A broad smile lit up his face. "It certainly did. You're a very lucky woman."

She nodded. "There are so many people I need to thank. You most of all."

"Not most of all. Without a donor, this wouldn't have been possible."

"I know."

"Before I let you talk to your husband, would you like to meet your donor?"

"Meet?" she cried softly. "But Mamma and I thought someone must have…died."

"No. In your case this altruistic donor is very much alive and came through the surgery beautifully, too. He wanted to see the person who received his kidney, but we'll only wheel him in for a moment."

Now that the transplant was over, the reality of the situation was overwhelming. She was about to meet the person who'd willingly given up a kidney for her? Clara couldn't comprehend that kind of sacrifice. Not really. What did you say to someone who'd just granted you a longer life?

Tears from too much emotion blurred her vision as she saw a woman pushing a man in a wheelchair. They came closer until she was able to make out his features.

It was the handsome face of her beloved husband.

She cried out his name on a sob. *"Why did you do it? Why?"*

"Don't you understand yet?" He was pushed as close to her as his wheelchair would allow. His intelligent brown eyes blazed with light. "I'm in love with you, darling. I think I was in love with you when we were children, but didn't know it."

To finally hear those words from that deep, silken voice…

More tears flowed down her cheeks. "I've been in love with you forever, but what if something happens one day and you'll need the kidney you gave me?"

"Then I'll give him one of mine."

Clara lifted her eyes to the woman who'd just spoken and received a second shock. "Isabella—" She hadn't realized.

"Yes." His sister smiled. "And if I find I need one, then Cristiano has pledged his to me. Because of you, Clara, our brother has found his happiness at last. This is what families are for, right? The Rossettis and the Casalis stick together."

On the fifth morning Valentino finished showering in preparation for leaving the hospital. Since their surgeries, he and Clara had been walking together, doing all kinds of exercises. They were more than ready to go.

Dr. Arno made his rounds after breakfast and released them. Within the hour a hospital van would be driving them back to Monta Correnti. This day seemed to have taken forever to get here.

As he was pulling on his tan chinos and a blue sport shirt he heard her call to him but it sounded muffled. He couldn't tell if she was excited or upset about something.

He emerged from his bathroom on a burst of adrenalin and found her standing by his bed.

"Look!" She turned around, giving him an eyeful of her womanly figure. All the tubes and catheters were gone. No more IV stand. She looked incredible and was dressed in the same outfit she'd worn to the track in Monaco. Those green eyes glowed as if they were on fire.

"Your kidney's been working inside me from the time it was transplanted. No more dialysis!"

It was the best news he'd ever heard. He took another step and wrapped his arms around her, careful not to apply too much pressure while their incisions were healing. "I'm glad I've been good for something around here," he teased to cover his emotions.

"Oh, Tino, I'm so happy and so terribly, terribly in love

with you!" She raised her hungry mouth for his kiss. They were starving for each other. Dr. Arno had told him they had to wait two weeks to make love. Valentino didn't know how he was going to hold out that long, not with a wife as passionate as Clara, but her comfort had to come first.

They had other rules to follow. Exercise every day. Walk. The longer the walks, the better. No driving a car or motor scooter for three weeks. No heavy lifting until after four weeks.

The fear that her body might reject his kidney had plagued both of them, but no longer. Naturally there was the possibility it might be rejected months or years later, but he refused to think about that right now. The different drugs she was taking were working.

"Signor Casali? Signora? When you're ready, the van is waiting for you at the south entrance downstairs."

Clara pulled away from him in embarrassment. Her face had gone a charming pink color. He would never tire of looking at her. Valentino had definitely come down with a serious case of love for his wife.

The nurse had brought two wheelchairs.

"Do we have to use them?" Clara asked her.

"It's hospital policy."

"Oh, all right," she grumbled and sat down in one. Valentino sank into the other one and reached for her hand. When she looked at him, they both saw the humor in their predicament and started to chuckle. Soon she was laughing. The sound filled him with an excitement he'd never known in his life.

After a short elevator ride, they were wheeled out to the van. The interior felt nice, comfortable. They thanked the staff for everything. Soon the attendant closed the sliding door and they were sealed off from the world for a while.

She darted Valentino a mischievous glance. "I feel like I did when we were little children. I would wait and wait for the end of school so I could run outside and hide from you. Somehow you always found me when nobody else could."

"It wasn't that hard." He grinned. "Whenever I got close, your laughter gave you away. I was attracted to it."

"My laugh?" she asked in an incredulous voice.

He nodded. "It has a happy quality. I liked being around you because of it. Don't ever stop. I couldn't take it."

"*Tino*—"

They were seated across from each other. He wanted to pull her onto his lap, but he didn't dare. After the hell she'd lived through, the thought of anything happening to her before they reached home was anathema to him.

Being a race-car pro, he had a problem letting anyone else drive him. The one hair-raising experience with his wife had been the exception because he adored her. At the moment he needed to have faith in the van driver's skill.

Since he couldn't hold her in his arms right now, he decided this would be a good time to tell her what Isabella had written in her e-mail. He already knew what Clara's response would be. She was a peacemaker. How else would she have survived from birth with a twin like Silvio?

Valentino's relationship with her brother still needed work. It would make her happy if he found a way to ease the tension. He'd have to think about that one.

"Tino?" she called out some time later. "Forgive me for interrupting you, but the driver's going the wrong way. He should have turned north."

"That's true, *if* we were headed for the villa."

"But we're not?"

"I thought we'd do something different."

For once she looked baffled. "Are you taking us to your old house on the lake?"

"No," he drawled.

She made a sound in her throat. "To the farm?"

"That depends on which one."

Silence fell between them before her gorgeous eyes rounded. "You bought the Brunello farm—"

His lips twitched. "Since the day we walked around the property, it's been known as the Casali place."

"Oh, darling—"

They were driving up to the farmhouse now. Her head swiveled around. "There must be a dozen trucks parked outside. My whole family's here! Whose car is that?"

"Isabella's. She brought Papa. He won't be able to stay long, but he came because he loves you."

"I feel the same way about him, Tino. He raised you as his own. I love him for that."

Valentino loved her for saying it and believed it. "They've all planned the celebration we couldn't have on our wedding day. Welcome home, *innamorata*."

She buried her face in her hands. In the next breath she'd broken down in quiet sobs from too much emotion. Valentino could relate.

He heard the van door open. Instead of the driver standing there, it was Silvio. His gaze shot to Clara, then passed to Valentino. For those few seconds he sensed her brother felt unsure of himself.

Taking advantage of the unexpected moment Valentino said, "Why don't you help her in the house while I talk to the driver?" He undid his seatbelt and climbed out of the van in order to give them some time alone.

Noise from the house reached his ears. Only the sounds of a big, gregarious family enjoying themselves could fill the air like that. By marrying Clara, he had entrée into their exclusive club. He'd never thought this kind of happiness could be his.

* * *

"Clara? This is for you." Bianca handed her a gaily wrapped gift.

"Another present? Thank you."

"Don't let Valentino open it," she whispered, kissing her cheek. "I'll call you in the morning."

Bianca, whose morning sickness seemed to be letting up, was the last of Clara's family to walk out the door. They'd brought the food and had done the dishes. Her mother had to be the one who'd made up their bed.

After her sister had gone, Clara, still seated on the couch, looked around the living room. She felt sated with food no longer forbidden to her. The wedding presents had been piled high on the coffee table. She couldn't wait to open them, but exhaustion had caught up with her. Tomorrow would be soon enough to dig in.

Seven o'clock wasn't late, but, having just gotten out of the hospital, she was ready for bed and knew Valentino was, too. A little while ago she'd seen him step outside with Silvio. She couldn't help but wonder how they were getting along. Maybe it was a good sign that her husband hadn't come back in yet, but it couldn't be good for him. He'd already been on his feet too long.

On her way to the bedroom with Bianca's gift, her gaze wandered around. Valentino had arranged for the interior of the house to be painted an off-white. He'd had it furnished with enough things for them to get by on. In a quiet aside he told her that, as soon as she was well enough, he expected her to decorate it the way she wanted. "Buy whatever else you want to make this *our* home, *piccola*."

Valentino was a rare man. It frightened her how much she loved him.

After she'd prepared for bed, she opened the present. Inside the tissue lay a black nightgown with lace straps. Definitely decadent.

When she'd asked Dr. Arno about that he'd said, "Two weeks and not before!" That was still nine days away. She smiled to herself before hiding it in the bottom of the drawer under some other clothes. Then she got in bed.

In a minute she saw Valentino's silhouette in the doorway. "We've got a slight problem, *piccola*."

Her heart skipped in worried reaction. "Silvio?"

"No. Amazingly enough he thanked me in a choked-up voice and we talked farming. I told him I would need his advice on how to go about getting started outside. He has offered his services. I never thought I'd see the day."

Contentment washed over her. She let out a relieved sigh. "Neither did I. Come to bed."

"That's the problem. In the hospital I would have sold my soul to be able to hold you. Now that I can in the privacy of our own bedroom, I'm telling you it wouldn't be a good idea."

"Yes, it would. We're both too tired."

"That's how much you know," he muttered.

"I'm wearing the same robe I wore at the villa."

"You think that protects you?" He started getting ready for bed. "Don't you realize how enticing you are when you're buttoned up from hem to neck?" he called out from the bathroom where he was brushing his teeth. "You might as well be wearing a sign that says 'warning—to proceed beyond this point could give you a heart attack'."

Clara laughed so hard it made her incision hurt.

When he finally climbed under the covers, they both lay on their backs. It was the most comfortable position for them. She reached out to touch his arm. He caressed hers. When his fingers came in contact with her graft, the movement stopped.

She heard Valentino suck in his breath. "Now I know why the good doctor left it in. He's a very wise man. You're safe from me for a while longer. *Ti amo*, Clarissima."

"*Ti amo*," she whispered back. It was liberating to be able to tell him *I love you*.

* * *

"What do you think, Papa? You're a connoisseur." Valentino had just dropped off Clara at the clinic for a checkup. Now was the perfect time to come to the apartment while he waited. He suggested the two of them sit at the dining-room table to enjoy a drink.

His father took another swallow. "It has a sweet bite. Very unusual."

"Do you feel it's good enough for your Rosa clientele to add it to the drinks menu?"

Luca eyed his son intently. "I didn't know you'd developed a taste for limoncello."

"In the last month I've developed a taste for several new things."

His father smiled at him. "Marriage obviously agrees with you. I knew it would once you found the right woman. That's the trick."

That *was* the trick.

"You're one of the lucky few who married your best friend and fell in love with her, too. That doesn't happen to everyone. I've a feeling it will last forever. It's a rare occurrence, just like this tangy liqueur." He lifted the wine glass and smelled the bouquet before emptying it.

"You've hit on the right word, Papa," Valentino mused aloud. Clara was like the drink she'd created. She had her own tang, her own flavor. His giving wife was no imitation of anyone else.

"Who makes it? This doesn't smell or taste like it came from Sorrento. It's sweeter."

"Your 'nose' never fails you. This comes from a local source."

"Ah… I knew it."

Among the traits he admired about his father was his insistence on sourcing local produce even if it was more expensive. He paid his staff more and gave them longer holidays.

These were the reasons he was in debt, but, on the other hand, these were the reasons the staff had stayed loyal to him. Giorgio had confided that Lisa had tried to bribe him several times to come and work for her restaurant, but she'd underestimated her brother's influence.

Luca stirred in his chair. "Do I know them?"

"Yes. Quite well, in fact."

He looked surprised. "They've never approached me."

Valentino smiled inwardly. "No. They wouldn't."

"What's their brand name?"

"Limoncello Clarissima."

His father blinked. "How unusual, yet beautiful… Reminds me of your wife. I hope she can one day give you a child because you'll have the most beautiful children around. But more importantly, I have to tell you that you'll make the best kind of father."

A lump lodged in Valentino's throat. "If such a miracle happens and it's a son, Clara has already decided we'll name him Valentino Casali in honor of your heritage."

"Well…" His father had to clear his throat several times. "Where did you say these people live?"

This was fun. "Right here in Monta Correnti."

"Why don't you bring them around to the restaurant tomorrow afternoon or the next afternoon and we'll talk about serving it for a trial period. I can't guarantee anything, of course."

"Of course," Valentino echoed.

He couldn't wait to get back to the farm to tell her. The long wait was finally over. Tonight would be their real wedding night. His papa had just made it possible for Valentino to give her a wedding present she'd never forget.

"About your idea for the tour-bus crowd. I think we should try it and see what happens."

Elated, he got up to kiss his father on both cheeks, then disappeared out the door with the bottle. There was only a little liqueur left. Enough to celebrate her return to life.

Once he took off in the Ferrari, it didn't take long to pull up outside the clinic where she was getting her post-op checkup. He hurried down the hall to the dialysis department. To his frustration she hadn't come out yet.

"She's not here," the receptionist called out. "She told me you were to meet her in the restaurant at the San Gallo hotel."

"*Grazie.*"

He had to fight his disappointment that they couldn't simply drive back to the farm. The San Gallo was the best five-star hotel in Monta Correnti and sat on a hill with its own lovely view. But it was always crowded, especially at this time of year when students and tourists were on spring break. Valentino didn't want to face hordes of people right now. All he wanted was Clara.

"*Buon giorno*, Signor Casali," the maître d' greeted him ten minutes later. "Congratulations on your marriage. I will give you a view table as soon as I can make the arrangements."

"Thank you, but that won't be necessary. I'm looking for my wife. She asked me to meet her in here."

He shook his head. "She hasn't come. No reservation was made."

Valentino took a deep breath. "I'll check with the concierge."

When he asked about her at the desk, the man said, "Signora Casali is in room 152. She'll be happy to know you've come. She was most anxious. Here's another key."

Filled with alarm that something had gone wrong at her checkup and she'd decided to tell him over their meal, he took the card key and raced across the foyer to the stairs. By the time he could let himself in the room on the next floor, his anxiety bordered on terror for fear her kidney had suddenly stopped functioning.

"Clara?" he cried out after flinging the door open.

"*Caro*—" she called from the bathroom "—I thought you would be at your father's longer."

"What's wrong?" he demanded.

"Nothing. I'm fine. I'll be out in a minute."

"You left the clinic without me. You're *not* fine! I know you're not." He raced across the room to open the door, but it was locked.

Frantic, he pressed his forehead against it. "*Piccola*? Don't shut me out."

"I would never do that."

He heard a click, then the door opened.

A barefooted woman stood before him. Except for her eyes that dazzled him with their green fire, nothing else was familiar. A new jasmine fragrance assailed him. Her dark hair was curly like a Gypsy's. She was a vision in sheer black lace over alabaster.

Her seductive smile captivated him.

"You have permission to discover for yourself that there's absolutely nothing wrong with me, *signore*." She wound her soft arms around him and gave him a kiss to die for. "But first, why don't you get out of these clothes? You've been my fantasy for years. Now I want the reality."

Valentino couldn't talk. He couldn't breathe.

"Is that going to be a problem for the famous Valentino Casali?" she teased. "Because if it is, you're in *real* trouble with your farmer wife."

MILLS & BOON®

JUNE 2010 HARDBACK TITLES

ROMANCE

Marriage: To Claim His Twins	Penny Jordan
The Royal Baby Revelation	Sharon Kendrick
Under the Spaniard's Lock and Key	Kim Lawrence
Sweet Surrender with the Millionaire	Helen Brooks
The Virgin's Proposition	Anne McAllister
Scandal: His Majesty's Love-Child	Annie West
Bride in a Gilded Cage	Abby Green
Innocent in the Italian's Possession	Janette Kenny
The Master of Highbridge Manor	Susanne James
The Power of the Legendary Greek	Catherine George
Miracle for the Girl Next Door	Rebecca Winters
Mother of the Bride	Caroline Anderson
What's A Housekeeper To Do?	Jennie Adams
Tipping the Waitress with Diamonds	Nina Harrington
Saving Cinderella!	Myrna Mackenzie
Their Newborn Gift	Nikki Logan
The Midwife and the Millionaire	Fiona McArthur
Knight on the Children's Ward	Carol Marinelli

HISTORICAL

Rake Beyond Redemption	Anne O'Brien
A Thoroughly Compromised Lady	Bronwyn Scott
In the Master's Bed	Blythe Gifford

MEDICAL™

From Single Mum to Lady	Judy Campbell
Children's Doctor, Shy Nurse	Molly Evans
Hawaiian Sunset, Dream Proposal	Joanna Neil
Rescued: Mother and Baby	Anne Fraser

0510 Gen Std LP

MILLS & BOON

JUNE 2010 LARGE PRINT TITLES

ROMANCE

HISTORICAL

MEDICAL™

0610 Gen Std HB

MILLS & BOON®

JULY 2010 HARDBACK TITLES

ROMANCE

A Night, A Secret...A Child	Miranda Lee
His Untamed Innocent	Sara Craven
The Greek's Pregnant Lover	Lucy Monroe
The Mélendez Forgotten Marriage	Melanie Milburne
Sensible Housekeeper, Scandalously Pregnant	Jennie Lucas
The Bride's Awakening	Kate Hewitt
The Devil's Heart	Lynn Raye Harris
The Good Greek Wife?	Kate Walker
Propositioned by the Billionaire	Lucy King
Unbuttoned by Her Maverick Boss	Natalie Anderson
Australia's Most Eligible Bachelor	Margaret Way
The Bridesmaid's Secret	Fiona Harper
Cinderella: Hired by the Prince	Marion Lennox
The Sheikh's Destiny	Melissa James
Vegas Pregnancy Surprise	Shirley Jump
The Lionhearted Cowboy Returns	Patricia Thayer
Dare She Date the Dreamy Doc?	Sarah Morgan
Neurosurgeon . . . and Mum!	Kate Hardy

HISTORICAL

Vicar's Daughter to Viscount's Lady	Louise Allen
Chivalrous Rake, Scandalous Lady	Mary Brendan
The Lord's Forced Bride	Anne Herries

MEDICAL™

Dr Drop-Dead Gorgeous	Emily Forbes
Her Brooding Italian Surgeon	Fiona Lowe
A Father for Baby Rose	Margaret Barker
Wedding in Darling Downs	Leah Martyn

MILLS & BOON

JULY 2010 LARGE PRINT TITLES

ROMANCE

Greek Tycoon, Inexperienced Mistress	Lynne Graham
The Master's Mistress	Carole Mortimer
The Andreou Marriage Arrangement	Helen Bianchin
Untamed Italian, Blackmailed Innocent	Jacqueline Baird
Outback Bachelor	Margaret Way
The Cattleman's Adopted Family	Barbara Hannay
Oh-So-Sensible Secretary	Jessica Hart
Housekeeper's Happy-Ever-After	Fiona Harper

HISTORICAL

One Unashamed Night	Sophia James
The Captain's Mysterious Lady	Mary Nichols
The Major and the Pickpocket	Lucy Ashford

MEDICAL™

Posh Doc, Society Wedding	Joanna Neil
The Doctor's Rebel Knight	Melanie Milburne
A Mother for the Italian's Twins	Margaret McDonagh
Their Baby Surprise	Jennifer Taylor
New Boss, New-Year Bride	Lucy Clark
Greek Doctor Claims His Bride	Margaret Barker